...ATCHED

Nicholas Fisk is the author of many popular books for children, including *The Talking Car*, *The Backyard War* and *Leadfoot* for Macmillan. He has worked as an actor, journalist, musician, editor and publisher, before becoming a full-time writer. He is married with four grown-up children, and lives in Hertfordshire.

SNATCHED

Nicholas Fisk

MACMILLAN
CHILDREN'S BOOKS

First published 1983 by Hodder and Stoughton Children's Books

This edition published 1995 by Macmillan Children's Books
a division of Macmillan Publishers Limited
25 Eccleston Place, London SW1W 9NF
and Basingstoke

Associated companies throughout the world

ISBN 0 330 33815 3

1 3 5 7 9 8 6 4 2

A CIP catalogue record for this book is available from
the British Library

Phototypeset by Intype, London
Printed by Mackays of Chatham PLC, Kent.

CHAPTER

CHAPTER ONE

THE SNATCH

'Shut up! Stay still!' the man hissed. Even those four words betrayed him: he was speaking a foreign language, not his own. 'Stay still!' he hissed right in Gemma's ear – she felt the heat of his breath. His hand gripped her neck like a clamp. She tried to kick him and could not reach. She tried to yell but he slipped a band of stuff – velvet? – over her head and into her mouth, gagging her.

Gemma struggled all the harder but it made no difference: he was pushing her towards the camper van. It was brown and beige outside; bright and holidayish inside. There were coloured stickers on the windows.

A girl had seized Gemma's brother, Mo. 'Make a noise and I'll break your wrist,' the girl told Mo. She was not big but she was amazingly hard and strong. She had his left arm bent right up between his shoulder blades. Her other arm was round his neck, choking him. Mo wanted to yell;

he could only gasp and splutter. He could smell her jumper. Musty, sweaty.

He lifted his right leg and brought his heel down hard on her foot. He heard her gasp with pain – good! – but she gave his wrist an extra jerk. Agony. He bit her arm through her thick sweater and opened his mouth to shout.

Instantly, she slipped the noose over his head and pulled it tight in his open mouth, gagging him. Thick, soft, velvety. He shouted against it but the sound was ridiculous. Nobody would hear it. Attempting to bite through the material, he bit his own cheeks. There was a taste of blood and the prickle of tears. She'd think she'd made him cry—

'In there,' she said. 'Quick!'

She thrust him towards the camper van. He dug his heels into the gravel. Even now he had time to notice how clean the gravel was, how neatly raked – how bright the flower-filled urns were on either side of the Embassy's great mahogany doors – how the sun glittered on the Embassy's window panes. There were people inside the Embassy, lots of people who knew them. Surely someone must see, someone must do something? He pushed and bucked and scrabbled with his feet.

He saw Gemma was already half in and half

2

out of the camper van, her legs thrashing. And then he was in, thrown in head first, and the sliding door was being slammed against his left leg. The girl said, 'Get your leg in, fool!' The door slammed shut.

The engine revved. The camper van began to move. It eased away smoothly, its tyres gently crunching the gravel. 'Professionals,' Mo thought. 'Amateurs would have made more noise.'

Already they were through the big wrought-iron gates. When they were in the main road, away from the Embassy, surely someone would notice?

There was another man in the camper van. This man grunted, 'Come here,' and flung his heavy arm round Mo's throat. His other arm was round Gemma's head and neck. Big man. Huge. Big face, even bigger neck. Suntanned arms, golden brown, covered with thick golden-red hair. 'Settle down,' this man said, tightening his arm so that the biceps bulged against Mo's ear and the hairs made his nose itch.

The girl was in the front, beside the driver. The driver was the fourth member of the gang: a lank, lean, dark, spectacled man. Early thirties. He turned round and said something amazing: 'Smile!' he said. 'You're supposed to smile!'

The huge man immediately smiled. He even began to sing a song, a TV jingle. 'What's the treat we all love best? Creamy, rich Munchmallow!' he sang, and beamed at the children. First at Gemma, locked in his left arm: then at Mo, trapped in his right. His great arms hid their gagged mouths.

Mo thought, Of course. He's playing at Jolly Uncle. Jolly Uncle with two kiddies, a playful romp. Family jaunt to the country – serious, responsible driver; a nice, country-fresh young woman and this Jolly Uncle, keeping the kiddies amused. That's what everyone would see.

'Creamy, rich Munchmallow!' sang the leader of the gang, the one who had seized Gemma. He was the leader because he had given all the orders – quiet, definite orders, just murmurs. He was leaning over the back of the seat where Gemma, Mo and the huge man sat. They couldn't see him, but no doubt he was smiling too. Happy families.

The camper van was being driven steadily and smoothly along roads familiar to Gemma and Mo. They had lived in the London Embassy for nearly a year and a half. They often travelled with their father, the Ambassador, in various cars. And with their English mother when she was in England. But mostly she stayed in their

Switzerland home, filling the house with music and musicians. Their parents were happy together, happy apart.

Chelsea, Mo thought. That's where we're heading!

But at Sloane Square, the camper van changed direction several times and suddenly they were in unfamiliar streets. Then the sun was behind them, they were heading north – not through the parks – was this Paddington? – and later, Mo and Gemma were completely lost. Steadily and safely the camper van took them further and further north, perhaps north-west. They caught glimpses of tree-tops, roofs, power lines. Nothing they saw meant anything. Even the sounds of other traffic were dying away. No traffic lights, no two-way traffic. They were on a small, feature-less road. Could be anywhere. Nobody smiled or sang any more.

The camper van braked, slowed, stopped. The girl got out. There was a metallic crash somewhere in front, then a rumbling, grating noise. The driver shouted out of his side window, 'Lined up OK?' and the girl's voice answered, 'OK'. The driver engaged first and the camper van charged a very steep and short slope. The sun went out, replaced by a mellow, amber light.

The driver put on the camper van's handbrake

and switched off the engine. The girl's voice, behind them now, shouted 'OK, I'll close up.' Doors grated and slammed behind the camper van. Bolts went home. The huge man's arms loosened their grip on Gemma's and Mo's necks. When they pulled at their gags, he did not stop them.

'Where are we?' Gemma demanded, when she was free of her gag.

'Furniture van.' He wiped his arms on his shirt to get rid of the dribble from the children's mouths. When you are gagged, you dribble.

'What are you going to do with us?' Mo said.

'It's already done,' the girl said. She was back in the camper van. There was room for her to get in and out because the camper van's doors slid, instead of opening out sideways.

'You're kidnapped,' the girl said. 'Snatched.'

Hearing the words said was bad – worse than suffering the act. Mo felt his stomach grow cold, Gemma began to look like a cat being taken to the Vet: she seemed to shrink restlessly, yet be ready at any second to expand and spring and cause havoc. Mo hoped she would not try anything. They were inside a tin cage inside another tin cage, surrounded by people twice their weight, size and age. His stomach grew colder.

'You'll never get away with it,' he told the tough-looking girl.

'Oh yes we will,' the girl said in a hard voice.

'But you won't!' Mo persisted. 'All you've done is build yourself a heap of trouble. You don't just crash in and kidnap people like us. There were plenty of others around when you did it. Someone must have seen you, seen everything!'

The leader of the gang interrupted. 'Excuse me,' he said, leaning forward and looking interested, 'this word "snatch", it means "to take hold quickly, to grab", is that not right? Yes, that is right. But we did not grab you quickly and without thought, not at all. The operation was most carefully planned, after a long period of close observing.'

Over his shoulder, the driver said 'Close *observation*.'

'Close observation, thank you. As I say, we planned everything most carefully. The secretarial staff of the Embassy: they have their coffee or tea in the morning always at the same time, is that not so? The junior staff go to the trolley in the corridor, so they are not near the windows. And the maintenance staff, they go to the little canteen in the basement, always at the same time, correct? And some of the security

7

staff too; they should not, but they do it. We have been observing all of this for some time.'

'That still leaves the senior staff,' Gemma said. 'And drivers and delivery men and gardeners. Various people. Anyone might have seen. Even my father.'

'No, I think not,' the leader said. 'Your father is in Berlin today, is that not so, and then he drives himself to Paris. And next he goes to Ottawa for a little time. And the gardeners: they go to their greenhouse where they make tea over a little lamp—'

'Stove,' said the driver.

'Stove, yes, thank you. It is most important to have the words correct for a foreign language do you not think? Then you spoke of the many kinds of people who might have seen us. But the policemen, the "Bobbies", they have their habits too and we have learned about them. So you see—'

'I see, I see,' Gemma interrupted, rudely. 'Message received and understood. You had it all planned.'

'That is correct,' the man answered, earnestly.

Gemma turned her attention to her cheek and the girl. She massaged her cheek because she still somehow felt the gag – a nasty, furry feeling. She studied the girl and thought, She's really quite pretty. No, not pretty – good looking, in a hard sort of way. Small, muscular, wide-jawed, strong-boned. Even her straight black hair grew strongly. The sort of girl who wins marathons when young and gets leathery when old. The sort of girl who knows how to slap faces. A toughie. But how tough? Gemma decided to test her.

'Take us home, you stupid cow!' she spat at the girl.

Instantly, the girl hit Gemma across the face with the palm of her hand; and on the return stroke, Mo's face with the knuckles. The blows were violent, painful and shocking.

Gemma recovered first. She worked her mouth about – one cheek was scarlet from the blow – then spat in the girl's face.

The girl wiped the spittle off her face with a paper tissue and said, expressionlessly, 'I thought you were educated kids. Ambassador's children and all that. But I see you've got a lot to learn.'

Then she hit them again, just as hard, so hard that Mo, for the first time in his life, 'saw stars'. And Gemma had to repeat the word 'Tough . . . tough . . .' to help herself keep in the tears.

CHAPTER TWO

THE GANG

They drove on through the sunny, early-September afternoon and evening. It was stuffy. Opening the camper van's windows did not help because the camper van was inside the furniture van. The huge man smelled of after-shave; the driver, of cigarettes – he smoked occasionally in an old-womanish fashion, pursing his lips and frequently knocking off ash into the exact centre of the ashtrays. At the back of the camper van, the leader of the gang brewed coffee and its welcome smell drowned all the others.

Coffee loosened tongues. The girl said, 'You two'll be all right so long as you behave your-selves.'

'Or you'll hit us again,' Gemma said, with an edge to her voice. 'He'll hold us and you'll hit us.'

The girl shrugged, unbothered. Everyone silently drank more coffee. The leader, frowning anxiously, said, 'Seriously. We do not want bother. It is not in our interest to harm you. Do as Kat says, behave yourselves—'

'Kat?' Gemma said, raising one dark eyebrow. 'Is that her name? How do you spell it? B, I, T, C, H?'

Mo laughed, wishing he'd his sister's nerve, even as Kat's hand flashed at him on its return trip from Gemma's face. 'Your faces will wear out before my hand does,' Kat said, as if she were delivering a scrap of country wisdom.

To Mo's horror, Gemma began to cry. He wished she wouldn't but could not blame her. Kat had a hand like a leather mallet. He put his arm round Gemma and murmured, 'Gem? You OK, Gem?' She snuffled and leaned against him. He could feel her swallowing her sobs.

The leader spoke. He said, 'Seriously. It is all unnecessary, this slapping and hitting. If only you will behave yourselves . . .'

Speaks like a foreign-language teacher, Mo thought. Looks like one, too. Scandinavian or something. Well built body, earnest, strong face.

Gemma had stopped herself crying. She looked up and spoke to the leader. 'Her name's Kat,' she said. 'Right? Kat being short for what?'

'Katrina,' said the girl.

'Kat-reen-ah . . .' Gemma said, making each syllable a sneer. 'Hand me some tissues, Kat-reen-ah. You might want to make me cry again. And you don't want to get those dainty hands mucky on my face, now do you?'

Kat, expressionless, gave Gemma tissues.

Mo said to the leader, 'You haven't got a chance. Someone must have seen you taking us.'

'But nobody has followed us,' said the leader. 'No cars, no police. No, I think we are secure, Morris.'

Mo winced. He hated his Christian name. British kids thought it was 'Maurice' and teased him. They wouldn't believe 'Morris' was just his English mother's family name, used as a Christian name.

'Call me Mo,' he muttered. Then he said, 'How did you know my name?'

'We know everything about you,' the leader said. 'You, your parents. Everything.'

'And what's *your* crummy name?' Gemma asked the leader.

'My name is Per. P, E, R. It is a Danish name but I am not Danish.'

'Lucky Denmark,' Gemma said.

'I am a citizen of the world,' the leader continued. 'The world is my nation.'

'And kidnapping is your occupation?' Gemma said.

'Not at all,' said the leader. 'I do what I do

12

because I *must*. It is necessary. For the Cause.' He had a permanent frown between his brows, a deep little slit. When he spoke of the Cause, the frown deepened.

'The *Cause*...' Gemma drawled. 'I can imagine. Lots of lolly. Stacks of banknotes. Some cause!'

Kat raised her hard hand. Gemma offered her face. 'Hit me again,' she said. 'Go on! Strike a blow for the Cause!' Kat lowered her hand.

Mo stared at his sister's vivid, wicked face, her witch-black hair, her spiteful little nose dinted at the nostrils, her down-curved red lips. Good old Gemma, he thought. Fire-ball. I'm almost two years older than you, but you win. Well, not always... Well, sometimes... Well, anyhow, you're a goer. But cool it or they'll make you cry.

To prevent her pushing herself over the edge, he nodded towards the huge man and asked the leader, 'What's his name? Mr Universe?'

The leader said, 'No, not Mr Universe. But he is very strong. We call him Macko. It is a sort of joking nickname, you understand.'

'Macko, macho, ha ha, very funny, how subtle,' Gemma sneered. 'Aren't you being a little stupid, telling us everyone's names? I mean, shouldn't it all be Secret Society? Masks and false names?

Even false noses, I can just see Kat in a false nose—'

Mo hastily cut her short. 'Where are you taking us?' he asked the driver.

'And what's your name?' Gemma demanded.

The driver, who had never spoken except to check a road number with the leader, spoke over his shoulder. 'The name is Michael,' he said. 'We're nearly at our destination. It's a nice place but isolated. Hard to locate.' He creased the corners of his mouth into a small, sarcastic smile.

'Not that hard,' Mo said. 'We've been going all these hours at about 40 mph, therefore—'

'And journeying into the setting sun,' Gemma said. 'So romantic. Wales? Is it Wales? Do say it's picturesque old Wales!' She clasped her hands girlishly and made big eyes at the leader. He laughed uneasily. 'You are . . . "sending me up" ' he said, searching for the phrase.

'That is correct,' Gemma said, imitating his accent. 'I am sending you *up*. And the judge will send you *down*,' she said. 'For years and years and years. For kidnapping us. And I hope you rot.' Her voice began to break up on the last word. Mo feared she would cry.

There was a rangle-dangle-bangle as the furniture van juddered over the tubular steel of a cattle grid. There was a quite long, lumpy, lurching drive after the grid; then Michael said, 'We're there.'

CHAPTER THREE

HIDEAWAY

I t had once been a farmhouse, that was obvious even in the late evening darkness. The walls were thick and the windows deep-set and small.

'We get out,' said Per, the leader. 'Go in,' said Kat, pushing Gemma ahead of her. There was no longer any urgency in the commands. Obviously the gang had no fear of being overlooked or overheard.

'Crummy place,' Gemma said as she entered the house, her nose high in the air. It *was* crummy: faded posters on the rough, white-washed walls, various grimy chairs, a beaten-up solid-fuel cooker with hods of fuel standing in their own gritty spillings. The low, yellowish ceiling sagged. The whole big, irregularly-shaped room smelled of yesterday's cooking, stale air, musty furnishings.

The driver, Michael, scratched his long, dark, untidy hair; blinked through his unusually thick-lensed spectacles; and said 'We'll eat now.' He looked rather professorish but also cigarette-stained.

'No we won't,' said Gemma. 'Loo first.' Nobody answered here. She said, '*Well*, then? Where is the *loo*? You *have* a loo, I suppose? Or is this it?' She waved a hand at the room, eyes glittering, nostrils arched, head high. Mo chuckled to himself. Good old Gem.

Kat escorted Gemma to the toilet. Mo heard Kat say 'Here, hang on. Sleeping bags. Grab hold. One for you, one for him.'

'Later,' Gemma replied grandly.

The loo door slammed and Kat reappeared scowling, carrying two sleeping bags.

Kat took food from the oven. To Mo's surprise it smelled delicious: and was. Beef stew with excellent vegetables floating in it, knobbly wholemeal bread with lots of butter, good yellow cheese, rosy apples. Per opened a bottle of wine.

'I drink wine with my meals,' Gemma announced. 'So does Mo.' She held out her glass, her thin brown arm rigid. Per frowned but poured some wine. Gemma drank hers at a gulp, without pulling a face. Mo knew she hated wine.

'Radio,' said Per, looking at his watch. Of course: the news. They all listened. The first item was an ecology conference. The second was the kidnapping. It was given a lot of air time. A Chief

17

Detective Inspector spoke. The words 'Ambassa-dor' and 'Embassy' were mentioned frequently. The kidnapping story was rated more important than an air battle in the Near East, an inter-national money council, and the death of a motor-racing driver.

'You've boobed,' Gemma said, loudly and clearly, as Per switched off the set. 'You've made idiots of yourselves. You snatched the wrong people!'

'You've picked the wrong target,' Mo said, sup-porting her. Gemma was right, he knew, to take a high line – to be scornful, arrogant, unyielding. 'My father, the Ambassador, is a very important man—'

'Which makes *us* important,' Gemma said. 'You haven't a hope.'

'There are other important people,' Per said, not loudly. 'People who are important to *us*. Not privileged people, like your parents. Or like yourselves. Poor people, suffering people, people who are oppressed . . . We fight for them.'

As he spoke, the frown between his eyebrows deepened and his handsome face looked even handsomer in its quiet earnestness. Mo could think of no reply to Per's speech. Would Gemma find something to say?

He looked at her. Her lips were slightly parted.

She was staring at Per, her eyes darkly luminous. She said nothing.

Oh Lord, Mo thought, Oh Lord . . . I hope she's not off again.

CHAPTER FOUR

OFF AGAIN

O ff again ... Gemma was always going off again. That was her trouble, Mo thought, lying in his warm sleeping bag. He wanted to sleep but was too tired and worried. Gemma was not. By the bright light of the moon through the flimsy, ill-fitting curtains covering the barred window, he could make out her face, half-hidden by her hair. Fast asleep. Asleep and probably dreaming.

Dreaming of what? Of whom? Per, Mo thought. I hope it isn't Per. But I bet it is! He's just the sort of thing that starts her off again ...

It was the frown, he decided. That would be enough to start her off. She never went for completely healthy specimens of anything: there always had to be a flaw, an injury, a defect. When Father gave them both ponies, Mo was thrilled; Gemma vaguely pleased. She liked dressing up in riding clothes and having the policeman hold up the traffic so they could clip-clop across the

Bayswater Road – she liked all those bits, but the pony meant very little to her.

But when the pony hurt itself on a broken milk bottle, everything changed. Now, the pony, useless for riding, was perfect as an object of passion. The Passion Pony! Gemma wept over, doted on, groomed and overfed the Passion Pony.

Good thing the pony didn't have an interesting frown, Mo thought. A frown like Per's.

There had been newts, he remembered. Newts – this was two or three years ago – from the pond in the park.

'*Dead*!' Gemma had moaned, holding up the jam jar by its piece of string. The newts floated belly up. 'Dead, *dead*, DEAD!' she had cried, louder and louder. Eighty faces turned to the figure in the nightshirt. Eighty distinguished, beautifully dressed ladies and gentlemen of all nations were stopped in mid-action, wineglasses frozen in mid air, forks halted in front of open mouths.

'My newts are *dead*!' cried the nightdressed figure with the jam jar. 'And *you* sit there eating *salmon*!'

That was the night of the Embassy Ball, Mo remembered. The Japanese Ambassador, sorry for the little girl with the dead newts, kindly sent a kitten to her the very next morning.

21

The Passion Pony; the Nerve-racking Newt; and now, the Catastrophic Kitten.

The kitten had worms. Gemma had convulsions.

Pony, newt, kitten. There had been others too. And now Per. Per with his brooding frown, his handsome lock of coppery hair falling over his forehead, his talk of 'poor people, suffering people. We fight for them'.

If Gemma got a pash on Per, it would cause serious trouble. Gemma would cease to be a rebel, a plotter and planner of escape; and become instead a melting marshmallow.

'You fool, Gemma!' Mo said, out loud. He struggled out of his sleeping bag – his gloomy thoughts had made it seem stifling – pulled aside the little curtain and stared out through the barred window. Just as he thought. Farmland in the moonlight, acres of farmland. Barns over there, some tents – ah, holiday-makers, campers, they might come in useful! – a cottage in the distance. But mostly land, almost treeless. No good making a run for it by daylight, you would be seen. At night, you would get lost.

There was a mirror. He looked at his dark reflection in it. Long nose, like his sister. Narrow face. Dark hair. Big, anxious eyes. You've got plenty to look anxious about, he said to himself.

He consciously stood straight and tensed his shoulders. 'You're the older brother,' he murmured. 'All right, then. It's up to you.'

He got back in his sleeping bag, began to make plans and fell asleep in the middle of them.

CHAPTER FIVE

BODYBUILDER

'Look about as much as you like,' said the huge man, Macko, next morning. 'You like guns? Have a look at this one!' He patted a revolver tucked in his big leather belt. 'Or do you want to go walkies? Go on then. Door's open. Just walk out.' He was hanging from the beam outside the front door, hanging by the ends of his fingers; and pulling himself up and down, time after time. His massive biceps, the size of half grapefruits, bulged the fabric of his blue track suit. His breath went Whoosh-shish-whoosh. He exaggerated the noises. 'Go on, then,' he said. 'Explore. But remember the gun.'

'Can't get past you,' Mo said. For the man's body filled the doorway. Macko replied by opening his legs in a rigid vee. Mo walked through. Gemma was following him – when the legs clamped together, seizing her like the claws of a crab. She was pulled up and down with him. She thrashed about and gasped. Macko went on with his pull-ups – whoosh-shish-whoosh – and tight-

24

ened the grip of his legs until her gasps became choking noises. 'Mo!' she croaked.

Kat, clearing away the breakfast, watched and smiled calmly. 'That's right, Mo,' she said, 'you help her. Rescue little sister.'

Mo started punching Macko in the back. It was like punching a tractor tyre. The man laughed. So did Kat. 'Don't hurt yourself,' she told Mo.

Mo saw a meat skewer lying in the grass. The skewer had a bit of rotten string tied to it and was starting to rust. Using it like a dagger, he plunged the skewer into Macko's backside.

Macko shouted and let go the beam. Gemma fell from his legs in a heap. Mo waited to be hit.

He was not. Macko was interested only in the meat skewer. 'It's rusty!' he cried. He sounded appalled. 'Look, Kat! Rusty! Blood poisoning . . . Septic wound . . .!' His lower lip shook. 'Biocin,' he said. 'Get my medicine case, Kat. Quick! There's Biocin in it . . .'

He sat down – winced – stood up again – and Mo saw that he was actually trembling. Kat, unmoved, fetched Macko's medicine case. Its several compartments were neatly packed with jars, bottles and plastic containers. There was a place for everything and everything was in its place.

'Health crank,' Mo muttered. 'Interesting . . .'

'Quick!' Macko said. 'That one there, Kat! And some cotton wool! Hurry! Infection! Serious risk . . .'

He zipped open his track suit down to his navel, reached behind himself and applied the cotton wool pad to his injured backside. His face was earnest and absorbed. 'What a thing to do!' he accused Mo. 'Using a rusty implement like that! Rust harbours germs and viruses! Kat, give me two of those tablets, the jar with the red cap. Quick!'

Gemma, like Mo, watched all this closely. She stared at the medicine case and raised an eyebrow at Mo. To Kat, she said, 'Excuse *me*, but Macko told us to go for a walk. OK if we obey him?'

Kat stood uncertain. Macko said, 'Get rid of them. I've got to *examine* this wound . . . examine it *properly*. Get me a mirror, Kat. You kids, get out.'

They got out. When they were clear of the farmhouse, they laughed till they rolled about. Because they were most likely being watched, they laughed all the harder and longer. 'Hurt his poor botty,' Gemma piped piercingly. 'Poison!' Mo squeaked. 'Awful, drefful poison! Oh, doctor, don't let me die!'

There was a solid thump in the grass very close

by. Something shining stuck out. Mo and Gemma stopped laughing. Mo inspected the thing. 'Crossbow bolt,' he said in a hushed voice. It was so deeply embedded in the ground that he had a job to pull it out.

From a high window in the farmhouse, Kat's voice called to them. 'Mind how you go,' she said, clearly, unpleasantly. 'And be back in twenty minutes. OK?'

She held the crossbow so that Gemma and Mo could see it plainly. They could see the high-power binoculars round her neck too.

'Bolt,' Mo said, looking at the crossbow. 'Bolt – that's what *we've* got to do. Bolt.'

'How? Where? When?' Gemma said.

'Don't know,' Mo said, miserably. 'Wish I did. Haven't an idea. But at least I've got this.' He gave Gemma a glimpse of the crossbow bolt.

'So?' Gemma said.

'Might come in useful,' Mo said, sounding wise. 'It's a weapon, isn't it? There's all sorts of things in that house that might come in useful. All sorts of gear. I'm making a list.' He tapped his forehead. 'Keeping it up there.'

Gemma groaned, loudly. '*Gadgets* . . .!' she said.

'You and your gadgets!' They walked in silence, both in a huff.

It always made Gemma cross when Mo went on about gadgets. He seemed to think gadgets were . . . true: real and important things, not just gadgets. He'd brood for hours over advertisements and catalogues offering mini CD players, video games, virtual-reality outfits, even trick burglar alarms. Surrounded by his precious gadgets, he'd brood about the next gadget and the gadget after that. He was gadget-mad.

She despised him for it. If he cared about – well, animals, something real, something alive . . . She thought about animals and slipped into a dream of bright eyes, twitching whiskers and furry bodies.

Mo awoke her. 'That medicine case! All those patent medicines and Make You Strong tablets and Brewers' Yeast and health junk!'

'*Body-builder*,' Gemma said, scornfully. 'All muscles and no mind. All the same, he *is* strong. When he had his legs round me it was like . . . I don't know what it was like. And all the time pulling his weight and mine up and down, up and down. Wow. Strong, but *strong*!'

'Then there's Kat,' Mo said, 'she's real tough. And *good* at things. Physical things. Lifting heavy hods and grabbing just the right number of knives and forks out of a drawer. Always right first time.'

'She's all right with a crossbow,' Gemma said with a shudder.

'She doesn't like you,' Mo said. 'You want to watch that. Don't stir her up too much, Gem. I know she's a bully – she liked slapping you about – but she might have a soft side.'

'Stick a skewer in it when you find it,' Gemma suggested.

'No, seriously—'

'The driver, Michael, I don't understand about him. What's he for? And where's he gone? He wasn't at breakfast.'

'He went off in a car in the middle of the night,' Mo told her. 'At least, I suppose he did. I heard a car leave.'

'Ah,' Gemma said. 'I suppose he's the link between here and London, or whatever. A go-between. To negotiate the ransom and the hand-ing over and all that. Like they do on TV.'

'Handing over,' Mo said. 'I wonder how soon that will be? The quicker the better for all parties, I suppose. Get the money, hand us over and that's that.' He looked at his watch. 'Better get back,' he said. 'She said twenty minutes.'

He gazed about him, memorizing the lie of the land. The farmhouse was the only high point. He shook his head. 'Wherever we go, they can see us,' he told Gemma. 'We'll never get away on foot. Not unless someone helps us. Those tents and caravans . . .' He nodded at them. There were people in them all right. Washing on a line, smoke from a chimney.

A muddy Land Rover jolted towards them. Per drove it. He leaned out and said, 'Kat wants you back. She wishes you to help prepare lunch. You, Mo, are to pick vegetables and you, Gemma, are to lay the table. We must all share in the work, you understand.'

Mo saw Gemma's face. She was staring at Per and nodding very slightly in agreement with his words – even with the last words. Her eyes were bright. She held her hands behind her back, girl-ishly. Again Mo thought, *Oh Lord*.

Per engaged first gear, then had an after-thought. 'Oh, you are looking at the homes of the other people living on this estate, I think. This is a sort of commune, you understand. Everyone here knows about you. We share the same political views. And all agree with the course of action I have adopted. That is why we chose this site for your detention.'

He let in the clutch and the Land Rover went on its way. 'So they're all in it,' Mo said. 'Great, just great,' he added bitterly.

'Great,' echoed Gemma – in entirely the wrong tone of voice: her face was dreamy, her eyes followed Per in the Land Rover.

Mo kicked viciously at the thistle.

Gemma was off again. For sure.

CHAPTER SIX

THE CAUSE

Being prisoners seemed completely to change the rhythm of things. Before, when they were 'real' children leading their 'real' lives, time had taken its time. For whole seasons – years, even – Gemma and Mo found themselves in schools in Switzerland, Sweden, Britain, Canada, anywhere. They learned the necessary tags of languages, made friends, took up hobbies and came to terms with the latest Embassy and its staff. The Embassy was a place in which their father worked – or rather, from which he worked: for he seemed to radiate outwards from the latest centre, always travelling, always getting into or out of the long black Cadillacs and Rolls-Royces that took him to and from airports, always hurrying in, smiling, with the latest amazing presents . . . then hurrying out again with his cluster of younger, briefcase-carrying men at his heels, talking urgently in the language that Mo and Gemma hardly knew – English had become their 'natural' tongue. So that was Father: off again somewhere, busy again, be good, back soon.

Mo and Gemma were used to it, just as they were used to their mother's flashing, urgent, magical appearances. There would be fuss in the Embassy, new flowers in the bowls, servants running, telephone calls, tyres scrunching the gravel – and then she would appear, excited and exciting, fast-moving and slender. This time her hair might have gold tints in it and her costumes would be beiges and fawns and big gold jewellery pieces. Next time it might be all furs and long soft leather boots and coats and swinging chains of dull, silvery metals. Even her hair would be changed. Now it had silvery lights in it and she wore moonstones with her swirling, moonlit, mysterious evening dresses.

You got used to it. The parents were like shooting stars. Mo and Gemma lived by fixed stars – each other. Together, they explored and exploited the Embassy and its staff. Very soon, the place became home and the people, family. The past was just memories.

You might remember and talk about the real-cream chocolate truffles in Brussels. They were very special, lasted only 24 hours and even then had to be kept in a fridge. Mo and Gemma organized themselves an endless supply, straight from the shop. The shop-owner was afraid to offend the Embassy children.

In Ottawa, Gemma and Mo joined a real rough gang of kids who smoked real tough 'doped' cigarettes. The dope was bird seed. Sometimes the stench and horrible taste of those cigarettes came back to Mo from nowhere. When the little seeds caught fire, they crackled. Often the whole cigarette caught fire and then you had to remember to look disappointed.

Mo and Gemma remembered these things, but only as highlights. Their real lives were like chapters in a book; long chapters. But now they were kidnapped, time either jerked and hopped, or stretched itself endlessly, like well-chewed chewing-gum. Sometimes your heart raced with fury to escape, to do something. At other times, it seemed that you had been kidnapped for ever. Being kidnapped was the only way to live and the farmhouse was your only true home.

It was one of those stretched-out chewing-gum times now, after a big and good dinner cooked by Kat. Through the skimpy curtains you could see the sky darken. Inside the thick-walled living room, oil lamps cast their muddy, yellowed, soothing light. Unusually, Michael was there, dozing on the sofa. Kat was studying a street map of London between dashes into the kitchen.

Why was she studying the street map? Mo wondered, and came to the conclusion that it didn't matter. He was too full of food to worry and anyhow, she was gone again, back to the kitchen, clatter-bang-crash.

Per had talked all through dinner. Now his carefully chosen words were directed only to Gemma, who sat on two big cushions on the floor at his feet. Her arms were round her knees. 'This Cause of yours,' she said, 'I don't get it.' Her voice was quiet and enquiring. Mo wished it were aggressive.

'It is very simple, our Cause,' Per replied. 'But like many simple things, it becomes complicated.'

Gemma, her eyes large and faithful like a dog's, looked up at Per and said 'How can a simple thing be complicated?'

'Peace,' Per said. 'Now, there is an example. Everyone would wish for peace, is that not so? Yet there comes along a bad man – a dictator maybe – and he does bad things. So the peaceful people must go to the war. There must be fighting.'

'But that isn't your Cause,' Gemma interrupted. 'I mean, it can't be just about Peace or Ban the Bomb or Flower-people. You talk about fighting. What are you fighting *for*?'

Per's frown became deeper and more interesting than ever. 'It is a very simple thing we fight for,' he said. 'A simple and great thing. It is Justice! Justice for the poor and oppressed. Justice, to bring a future to those people who have no future. It is to *care and share*, that is how you say it, I think. To care and to share the good things of this Earth.'

'Gosh!' Gemma said.

'Tosh!' Mo said under his breath. He would have liked to have said it out loud, but realized that this was a good time to keep his mouth closed and his ears open. The more you knew about your enemy the better.

'I do see what you mean, I really do!' Gemma enthused. 'There are so many people in the world who have nothing . . . I've seen them, with my own eyes. But somehow I never thought about it, I just took it for granted—'

'Like those chocolate truffles in Belgium?' Mo said, unable to keep his mouth shut any longer. 'You took those for granted all right, Gem! Mouthful after mouthful, you really hogged them!'

Gemma stared him down with large, saintly, dark eyes. 'That was before I *understood!*' she said, nobly. Mo groaned and gave up.

'Belgium,' Per said. 'Brussels, yes? You were in

the Brussels Embassy with your parents? You have travelled much, is that right? So, in the Brussels Embassy—'

'The Embassy was fantastic!' Gemma said, gabbling to keep Mo out of the conversation. 'It was real old, sort of sandy-coloured stone, almost golden, with these terrific great windows and long polished wood floors inside and golden furniture and that. And huge Chinese vases, so big you could hide a person—'

'Pity you didn't fill them with truffles,' Mo said. Per and Gemma seemed not to hear him.

'And your father,' Per said. 'What was he doing in this place?'

'Oh, ambassador things, *you* know. The usual things. Big-deal politics and economics and defence. Things like that.'

'Tell me about those things,' Per said, leaning forward.

Ah, here it comes, Mo thought. Now we're coming to it. He's going to pump Gemma about the Embassy and what goes on in it. He's a revolutionary and he wants the inside dope, stuff he can use to help the Cause.

'I don't know I can tell you much,' Gemma said. 'I mean, politics and economics and that . . .' She shrugged her shoulders prettily. 'I guess I'm a bit young for that sort of thing,' she added, rolling her eyes and giggling.

'And so *cute*,' Mo added savagely, under his breath. He had a magazine open in front of him. He pretended to be reading.

'But your father is working very hard at the Embassy?' Per said. 'He has many duties and obligations, I think?'

'Oh, he works like crazy!' Gemma said. 'Wherever he is, he's always working on documents, or planning trips, or catching jets, or attending functions . . .' She made a puffing, Oh-gosh sound and rolled her eyes again.

'So he must have many helpers and assistants,' Per said. 'And cars at his disposal. Even, perhaps, a private aeroplane, yes? An executive jet, so that he may work and travel without interruptions?' He was leaning over Gemma, his face alight with interest.

'Why, no, he hasn't got a plane,' Gemma said; then paused, perhaps puzzled by the turn the conversation was taking. Why should Per, the revolutionary, the man with a Cause, be so interested in cars and aircraft and all the rest of it? That was what was puzzling her, Mo decided. He was puzzled too.

'He can always *charter* a light plane . . .' Gemma said, trying to be helpful to Per.

Mo thought, Of course! Revolutionaries blow things up. Particularly aircraft carrying VIPs. Per's thinking of planting bombs in aircraft, that must be it—

'These receptions and dinner parties,' Per said, still frowning with concentration, still leaning over Gemma. 'Are they very often?'

'Yes, I guess they are,' Gemma said uncertainly. 'I mean, in Brussels there were a lot, but in Ottawa Dad sort of does his homework most of the time. He just locks himself up and gets out his briefcase. That kind of thing . . .'

'A reception in an Embassy,' Per said, leaning back and frowning at the ceiling. 'That must be very grand, I think. There will be many courses of food and much fine wine to drink. And the ladies in their best gowns, with jewels . . . Oh, yes, a most impressive sight. And most of all when they arrive or depart in their limousine cars. The doors of the cars are opened by the servants, is that not right? Servants wearing liddery . . . special costumes, liddery . . . No, that is not the word . . .'

Kat bustled in and began putting away newly-washed dishes on the shelves of the dresser. 'Livery, not liddery,' she said, slapping the dishes into place with her usual slam-bang efficiency.

'Livery, yes, that is the word I was meaning,' Per said.

'*Livery*,' Kat said savagely. 'Rich people eating rich food served by able-bodied men wearing livery. People stuffing themselves – having trouble with their livers. Livers and livery. Euch!'

'Yes, yes, that is what I am meaning!' Per cried. 'The poor people, the starving people, they have nothing. All over the world there are such people! That is why—'

'I heard you asking about the Cause,' Kat said over her shoulder – she was still angrily putting away dishes – to Gemma. 'A kid like you wouldn't know about real things. Wouldn't want to know. So why pretend you're interested? You've got it all on a plate, haven't you? Daddy's *frightfully* rich and important and Mummy's *frightfully* busy worrying about her next hair-do or going on a special diet. While all over the world, there are people – real people – starving!'

Mo looked over the top edge of his magazine, studying each face in turn. Gemma sat upright now, no longer hunched in her little-girl huddle, her face strained and puzzled. Kat scowled at the plates, arched her strong spine and stuck out a scornful lower lip. Per looked handsome and earnest and noble and somehow out of place, temporarily out of things. Michael, on the sofa, gaped and made the beginnings of a snore.

Ah-hah, Mo thought. Ah-ha, oh-ho, hum-hum. A small, pleasant feeling of superiority warmed his brain. The feeling grew as he studied the faces. Weaknesses, he thought; they've all got their weaknesses . . .

Per broke the long silence. 'It is as she says,' he told Gemma. 'Just as Kat describes it. The weak and the poor suffer, always them. There is no caring and sharing, no justice. While the rich! – oh, the *rich!*' he sighed and shook his head. Gemma looked up into his face with eyes that were once again darkly melting. Kat bustled out.

'Yes,' Per said to her, 'there must be many very rich people at these Embassy affairs, I think. And tell me: when the servants in their livery have let the people in, what happens then? They are received by your mother and father, I expect; there is much shaking of hands, of course. But after that what do they do?'

'Well, they have drinks,' Gemma replied. 'Drinks are served, *you* know . . .'

'Ah, drinks. That would be champagne, I think? Or white wines? And little foodstuffs, the *canapés*, they are passed round, yes? And everyone converses, of course. The men in their evening suits with the decorations across the chest, and the ladies in their evening dresses and jewels. All looking their best, because it is a formal occasion, yes?'

Oh me oh my, Mo thought, whatever happened to the Cause – the good old noble Cause? When is Per going to get back to *that*?

'Often there is music,' Per said. 'Or so I understand. A little band plays, am I right? A string band, of course, very quiet and select so as not to disturb the conversations . . . Is that correct?'

Mo thought, Quite correct. And *I* won't disturb *this* conversation, Per, old man. Because it's telling me so much about you.

The warm feeling of superiority spread and grew inside him.

CHAPTER SEVEN

THE TUNNEL

Mo and Gemma began digging their escape tunnel.

It was a surprisingly safe operation. Their window was barred. The only entrance or exit to their room was by the short passageway into the big room. Mo and Gemma could hear anyone approaching.

Most of the time, only Kat was in the farmhouse. She was the person Mo and Gemma feared and disliked. But she was a radio addict. Her radio was always on. Its noise hid the noise Mo and Gemma made digging their tunnel.

The tunnel just might work: and in any case, it gave them something to do. It was a routine. Mo's bed, under the window, was pulled into the room; a chair was angled against the door to delay the entry of any intruder; the floorboards immediately under the window were prised up with the crossbow bolt (and later, replaced exactly as before); and the digging started. The crossbow bolt was the only tool at first. Later they found a garden trowel and fork. Then the digging went faster and faster.

'In those films, it's getting rid of the soil that causes the trouble,' Mo said.

'Lucky old us, then,' Gemma replied. 'We just chuck it out of the window . . . Like *this* . . . Out you go!' And another plastic-sack load was tipped out to disappear in the brambles and nettles outside. Their window overlooked the dead side of the farm, the place where bottles, ancient farm machinery, broken furniture and other clutter fought for space with weeds and grasses.

'We've even got our pretty little brush,' Gemma said, mincingly, and swept traces of spilled earth off the windowsill. 'Thank you, Kat . . .'

There had been a fight about the brush. Gemma, nostrils raised and flared, had demanded that her room be kept 'even half-way clean'. She had stared at Kat, raised an eyebrow and held out a broom and a brush to the girl. Kat replied by knocking Gemma off her feet with one backhanded swipe. 'Clean it yourself, you little madam!' she had shouted. 'And you can start now! Here!'

The brush was thrown at Gemma's head. It was exactly what was needed to clean up around the tunnel. Kat never noticed its absence.

While they worked, they talked. They tried to plan. It was very difficult. 'I mean, what do we really know?' Mo complained. 'And what good to us are the things we do know? It's not like the movies and telly. There, they make these terrific dashes, trying to avoid the spotlights—'

'And shoot-outs,' Gemma said. 'Big shoot-outs at the end. The baddies go blam-blam-blam and always miss, and the goodies go bang and always hit. Pity it's not like that for us.'

'Keep digging,' Mo said, 'and we'll go through the checklist again. What have *they* got and what have *we* got?'

'They've got a radio,' Gemma began. 'They keep in touch with Michael with it. But even if we could get to it, neither of us knows how to use it—'

'I know, I know,' Mo said. 'And they can use the phone. And they've got weapons.'

'The other things they've got,' Gemma said, 'are transport, friends, muscles, weight, communications – oh yes, and *us*. They've got us. So what have we got?' Her voice rose despairingly.

'Well, we've got quite a lot,' Mo said. 'I mean, there's the Police and Father, they won't just be standing about doing nothing—'

'We were talking about *us*,' Gemma said.

'All right then, *us*. We've got surprise on our

side. They know what *they* mean to do. In fact they've already done it. But they don't know *our* intentions.'

'Which are?'

'Well, there's this: the tunnel. When it's finished, we can get out . . . and perhaps we can get the Land Rover or one of the cars going. I mean, I can drive—'

'You can't,' Gemma said. 'You just know how, or think you do. You can't really drive.'

'Well, suppose we find bikes, then. Bikes would be good.'

'Suppose we grew wings and fly,' said Gemma, tiredly, and got on with the digging.

CHAPTER EIGHT

WINGS

Next day, the wings arrived.

It was Sunday and sunny and thundery-hot. As Mo said later, the big storm clouds must have caused the warm updraughts that carried the wings to their feet.

Mo and Gemma lay in the grass wishing they had swim-suits. Kat, fit-looking in a bikini, sat in a lounger and kept an eye on them. Macko, in a leather loincloth, exercised his pecs and abs, whooshing and hissing and sweating. Michael was absent again. Per hoed in the vegetable garden, frowning at the overgrown radishes and shot lettuces. 'We must all do our share,' Mo murmured to Gemma. She pretended not to hear.

The powered model aeroplane ambled lazily and silently in the sky, dipped a wing, met the cooler air rising from the field, and decided to come down.

It landed almost at Gemma's feet – stubbed its wheels in the long grass – tipped over on its nose – fell back again so that its tail was correctly on the ground – and glinted in the sun, asking to be admired.

It was something to admire. The wingspan was about a metre. The engine, Mo instantly saw, was a Tenko Meteor IIIb, carefully cowled so as not to spoil the scale effect of a three-seater cabin-cruiser design. The fuselage and wings were covered in red tissue decorated with silver sunray flashes. In the glazed cockpit, a little pilot, carved from balsa wood, sat proud and upright with his hands on the tiny control column.

Gemma gave an admiring, 'Wow!' Mo stared at the little aircraft in speechless admiration. Kat glanced lazily at it then kicked the wing with her bare foot – kicked it hard enough for her toenail to split the doped tissue of the wing-tip.

'You mean . . . stupid . . .' Mo began, chokingly. He got no further. Kat was instantly on her feet, hand swinging. 'What did you call me?' she kept shouting. She was furious.

The noise of the smacking blows distracted the distant Macko. He sprinted, puffing profession-ally, to the scene. 'What's going on?' he said. 'Where did that thing come from?'

'I'm just about to put my foot through it,' Kat grated.

'No, hold on!' Macko said. 'It's nice.' He touched the aircraft gently with his great brown fingers, admiring it. 'You shouldn't break a thing like this,' he told Kat. 'It's too *good* to break,' he explained. 'Let the boy have it.'

'All he's getting is another belt across the mouth,' Kat replied.

'You know, you're too free with your hands,' Macko told her. 'You want to lay off. Don't damage the goods, know what I mean?'

'I'll damage that plane,' she said.

'You won't. Here, Mo, take the plane. Go on, take it.' Macko had to hold Kat back while Mo picked up the plane and began walking towards the house with it.

He turned to look back when he heard the slap: one of Kat's crackers, he thought, a real hearty one. He was right. In her fury, Kat had hit Macko.

Macko rubbed his face with his left hand. He said nothing, just rubbed his face. Kat shouted something at him, Mo could not hear the words. High-pitched swear-words.

Macko's right hand seized Kat's left wrist, wrenched it upwards and bent it back so that it travelled in an arc over her ear. It kept travelling. She had to give way. Her knees bent and her back arched. Macko forced her to the ground, never letting go of her wrist. He knelt astride her. He started hitting her, carefully and scientifically.

Each time, she screamed. Her heels drummed. Mo and Gemma ran to the house, not wanting to see or hear.

Soon, Macko swaggered through the doorway. He was laughing to himself. Hur-hur, hur-hur. A contented sound. 'You can hang on to that plane, sonny,' he told Mo. 'It's yours, as of now. Hur-hur.'

Outside, in the distance, Mo and Gemma could see Kat's body. It rolled this way, then that, from one side to the other. Gemma said, 'I'll go to her, she needs—'

'You stay here,' Macko said. He was cleaning a shotgun. He glared down at Gemma. She backed away from him.

At last, Kat limped and staggered into the house. She had to cling to the table to stay upright. Mo and Gemma looked away. Macko eased himself back in the chair, stared at her, still cleaning the gun.

Mo and Gemma ran to their room and slammed the door. They did not speak or look at each other.

CHAPTER NINE

AIRSCREW

The plane, the plane . . .

Long after Gemma got tired of digging and dozed on her bed, Mo stared at the plane. There had to be a use for it.

Outside, voices from the big room interrupted Mo's thoughts. He listened at the keyhole. Someone might say something useful.

Kat: '. . . he beat me up, Per!' (so Per was there). 'Did a great job, I must say . . .' (an hysterical laugh). 'And he's given that kid Mo the plane. I ask you . . . Suppose he got it flying – stuck a message on it and got it flying—'

Macko: 'He can't do anything with the plane. Those planes use special fuel, what's-it-called – didn't you know that? Even then, they take hours to get started—'

Per: 'Listen, Macko, you must never again . . .' (he spoke so quietly that Mo could not overhear).

Mo sat back on his heels. 'Suppose he stuck a message on it . . . got it flying!' Of course! That was the thing to do! There wouldn't be much hope of reaching the right place and the right people, but there was *some* hope . . .

And besides, it was such a beautiful little plane. Better than anything he himself had ever made. Really professional. 'Chris. M. Meadows, tel: 736064'. That was the name on the neat little label stuck on the wing. You know how to build planes, Chris. Here's to you.

How to make it fly? Macko was right: getting the correct fuel was out of the question. So the motor would have to go. Another power source was needed. There was a power source somewhere, he remembered seeing it, it was a sort of picture in his mind. When? Where? What?

Suddenly it came to him – the octopus. No, the octopuses. There were two of three of them in the Land Rover – those brightly-coloured, fabric-covered, multi-strand rubber straps with a bent-metal hook at either end. To hold down loads.

A lovely source of power for a model plane. He'd dissect an octopus, take out the rubber strands, make them into the rubber motor. Easy.

But the airscrew, that was a problem. Rubber-powered models needed big airscrews, three times the size of the propeller in front of him. Difficult.

No, not difficult at all! He'd carve it. He'd done

it before. He could remember the wood blank, ready-printed with the right pattern, that came with his first flying-model kit. It was photographed in his mind.

But a knife. He had no knife.

No, wait: there were all sorts of knives among the farmhouse cutlery. Most were stainless steel: too soft. But hadn't there been a really old knife, with a plain steel blade – one of those knives that took a razor-like edge?

Footsteps in the corridor! Mo scrambled to his feet, Gemma woke up alarmed. But it was only Per, shouting, 'It is dinner time. You must both wash your hands then sit at table.'

Mo washed his hands in the kitchen, gently opened the cutlery drawer and saw half a dozen plain steel knives. He picked up the rustiest and most neglected-looking and slipped it in his pocket.

As simple as that.

Next morning, he found a carborundum sickle hone, long ago flung into a corner of the barn. That sharpened the knife.

He found a perfect bit of dried-out wood, light and soft and easily carved.

He began sketching and carving, thoroughly enjoying it; and kept his eyes open for wire to bend into a shaft; for scraps of wood, to reinforce the tail end and form a nose cone; for a strong, small dowel of wood to go through the reinforcement and hold the rear end of the motor; for

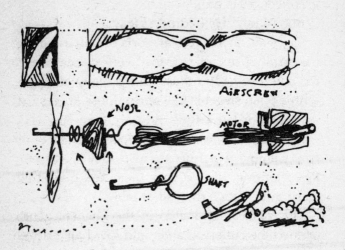

small washers to make smooth bearings for the airscrew when it spun against the nose cone. Everything was clear in his mind now. He destroyed his sketches.

It is amazing what you find when you keep your eyes open and know what you want. Within three days everything was finished.

When he showed his work to Gemma and explained his plan, she said, 'Who's a clever Mo, then?' and kissed him. He grinned.

CHAPTER TEN

THE WIRE

By the time Mo had almost completed the rubber-drive modifications to the plane, Kat had recovered from her beating. Now she was quieter, but just as vicious. She would begin laying the table – remember Gemma – and shout, 'Hey, you, you spoiled little brat (slap), finish this off (slap)! And you, Mr Ambassador's son, peel the right honourable potatoes (slap)'. The slaps were not what they used to be, however. They lacked the old meaty punch.

'She's in love,' Gemma explained to Mo when Kat was out of earshot. 'Haven't you noticed? She's even dieting. Not eating potatoes.'

'In love?' Mo said. 'Who's the unlucky man?'

Instead of answering, Gemma became suddenly confused. Her voice faded. She turned her head away.

'Oh, *I* get it!' Mo said. 'It's Per. Kat fancies Per and you fancy Per and you're all upset about Kat! Oh yes you are! You've got this child-bride dream, he's just about to sweep you into his manly arms when along comes his jungle bride, Katrina Queen of the Wild—'

'Shut up,' Gemma said, darkly.

But Mo was enjoying himself too much to stop. 'See her in her leopard-skin bikini!' he cried. 'Swinging from tree to tree, speeding on her way to her mate! While alone in the jungle hut, the child-bride waits – that's you, Gem! – all huddled up in a corner, with only her faithful chimp for company—'

'Chimp,' said Gemma, dimly. 'That would be you.' Then she started crying.

Mo moved to her. 'I didn't mean—' he began. She lashed at him with her hand and managed to hit his shoulder.

Kat came in, sternly, and said, 'Pack that in, you two, I do the slapping round here. Get the table laid.'

Mo met an unexpected and major obstacle in finishing the plane.

The wire shaft for the airscrew had to go through the noseblock and airscrew, then be bent into two separate and complicated shapes. At the front, there had to be a small, tight, three-quarters-of-a-square shape to bite into the wood of the propeller. At the rear, he needed a loop with a little cranked tail. The rubber motor would be held in this loop and then the tail would be sprung round the shaft to prevent the pull of the motor uncurling the loop.

The job needed pliers. But he had no pliers and could not ask for them. ('*Tools*? What do you want *tools* for?')

He explained the problem to Gemma. She listened, bit her lip thoughtfully and said, 'Wouldn't a penknife do? You know, those notches between the blades. They'd hold the wire.'

'But I haven't got a penknife,' Mo replied.

'Per has,' Gemma said, knowingly. 'Leave it to me.'

She walked off confidently leaving Mo scowling. 'Per,' he muttered. 'Oh yes, Per . . .' Per would look up when Gemma entered the room. His eyes would become interested. He would make room for her to sit near him and perhaps say something, anything, to start a conversation. She would sit close to him and they'd talk and talk.

Still scowling, he followed Gemma and silently watched her go to work on Per. It all happened as he knew it would. Soon they were talking, heads close together: talking in low, relaxed voices, as they always did.

And the conversation was the same as ever.

However it began, it always ended with talk about Gemma's past life – about the Embassy, the places Gemma had seen, the meals, the beaches, the airports, the famous people, the statesmen and celebrities. Per could never hear enough about them. Even now, he was at it again.

Mo listened to Gemma telling Per about a banquet. Constantly, he interrupted her with careful, earnest questions: 'That diplomat, he arrived in his own helicopter, you say? A big one? That must be very nice.' Or, 'It was a private beach, I suppose? Not for the ordinary people? Oh yes, it would be so. A special beach, quite private.'

Obsessed, Mo thought. Per's obsessed with money and grandeur and privilege and rank. And Gemma plays up to him. Now she's raving on about Rome, telling him lies. Rome was where she threw a tantrum when they served her half-melted ice cream. Bali was where I got sunburned and couldn't go swimming till the day before we left. Rio was where Gemma came out in a rash and Father's luggage got lost. But to hear her tell it – and to see Per listening, all bright-eyed and eager—

'Oh, and another thing,' Gemma said, interrupting his thoughts, 'can I borrow your penknife for a minute? It's got such a super little file,' she gushed. 'Just right for my nails. Please, Per!' She looked up at him with dark, soulful eyes. He handed her the penknife without a glance. 'And then you went to Morocco,' he said. 'That must have been most interesting. Tell me . . .'

Later, she handed Mo the penknife. He nearly ruined it bending the wire. The plates separating the blades were chewed and scarred. 'He'll notice,' he said, miserably. 'He'll see the marks and guess.'

'Oh no he won't,' Gemma said. 'Give it to me.' He handed her the penknife. She went back to Per – and cried, 'Thanks! Catch!' and threw the knife to him, deliberately throwing it wide. The knife hit the metal of the fireplace grate and clattered to the floor. 'Oh, stupid me!' Gemma cried, wide-eyed and distressed. 'Oh, I'm so sorry! I've spoiled your lovely knife!'

'It does not matter,' Per said, pocketing the knife without looking at it. 'Did you say your father once met Frank Sinatra? That must have been very interesting. So famous a man . . .'

Mo sneered heavily and inspected the wire shaft of the airscrew. The sneer faded. He had done a good job, a lovely job. He twiddled the airscrew, watching the twirling shaft glint, and forgot about Per.

CHAPTER ELEVEN

TAKE OFF

T he plane was ready for flight.

Mo had fitted weights in place of the airscrew and the two of them had run about playing what appeared to be childish games, throwing the plane to each other – but now it looked like a mere glider – and laughing a lot. Really, they were perfecting the glide.

'Yes, she should fly all right,' Mo said. 'But we've got to have the right weather. She won't get far without sun. She'll just go up and come down again. We need heat, like we had the other day. Sun, big clouds, thermals, updraughts.'

'And privacy,' Gemma said. 'Won't do much good if they see us launching the plane . . .'

'We'll create a diversion,' Mo said. 'Do something crazy while the plane is launched.'

'I could have one of my fits,' Gemma said. 'You know how good I am at fits.'

'Fits! What are you talking about? How do fits fit?'

'You'll see,' Gemma said, airily. She looked at

the sky. 'Come on, sun!' she said. 'Shine!'

It shone, brilliantly, next day. It was more like high summer than September. Morning mist rose from the fields and soared up to swell the first fluffy clouds. By afternoon, there was a shimmering heat haze over the fields, and the clouds were solid as cauliflowers.

In the late afternoon, Mo said, 'This is it. Just about perfect. And only Per and Kat in the house. Cross your fingers—'

'And my eyes,' Gemma said, crossing them hideously. 'It's time for my fit.'

'OK, then. Have a good froth.'

Five minutes later, Gemma foamed at the mouth. This was chewed soap. The rest was artistry. Her spine arched, her legs thrashed, her tongue stuck out, her eye-whites glared horrifyingly. It took both Per and Kat to restrain her, hold down her tongue with a spoon, and carry her inside the farmhouse.

While everyone was concentrating on Gemma, Mo launched the little plane. The same soap that made Gemma froth lubricated its fully wound rubber motor.

Its ascent was much too steep. It dug one wing down, turned sharply and hung on its airscrew while Mo prayed at it – 'No! No! Level out! Please!' It heard. With the first burst of power spent, it went into a dipping climb, each swoop a bit too steep, but it might be all right, it had to be all right.

The climb steadied. Now it was too high for Mo to read the messages on its wings:

SOS! HELP! SOS!
We are the kidnapped children
EMBASSY KIDNAP
Take this plane to Police Station NOW!

On the sides of the plane were detailed messages about the farmhouse; and about Gemma, Mo and their parents.

The rubber motor ran out and Mo held his breath. This was the moment that mattered. Either the glide was right or it wasn't. Either the plane fell out of the sky or it stayed up.

It stayed up. Better still, it found a warm up-current, a thermal.

It basked in the warm, rising air. It still dipped its nose now and then, alarmingly in Mo's eyes; but the plane was not worried. It began to perform long, lazy, left-hand circles interrupted by waverings and flutterings. But each circle was higher than the last. Mo began to realize that the little airborne thing, occasionally twinkling the sun's reflection at him, was firmly determined to stay up. It thought it was a proper duration model. In fact, it was a happy fluke. Almost a miracle.

And still it climbed.

From the farmhouse door, Kat called. 'Mo! Mo! Where are you? Come here! Hurry! Mo! Your sister!'

Reluctantly, Mo obeyed. 'She's very ill,' said Kat. She looked afraid and clumsy. 'Some sort of fit!'

'Not . . . *again*?' Mo said, wishing he could make himself go white. However, he knew he was good at the staring eyes and dropped jaw. 'Please . . .' he said, hollowly, '*take* me to her.'

Gemma had been laid on her bed. Her colour was wrong, too healthily pink and brown, but her brow was nice and sweaty and the rigidly clenched fingers were perfect. Mo knelt by her and pressed one of her hands to his lips. '*Speak to me!*' he said.

She replied with rasping breaths. She was strong on rasping, and practised often.

Kat said, 'What do you do when she's like this? Do you give her medicine?'

Mo replied, truthfully, that there was no medicine that could help her. 'Just leave her alone with me,' he said, bravely. 'I'm used to it.' Kat left, but not before Mo had tried another '*Speak to me!'* He thought it even more pathetic than the first.

The door closed on Kat. 'OK,' Mo whispered. 'Speak to me. Utter a syllable. Did you keep them all busy? Can anyone have seen me?'

'Busy as bees!' Gemma said. 'But I'm feeling a bit flaked. It's not easy doing fits, you really have to work at it. What about the plane?'

'You'd never believe!' Mo said. He made upward spiralling motions and beamed. 'Anything you want?'

'Water. I'm parched. Bone dry.'

CHAPTER TWELVE

LANDING

'Bone dry, man,' said Mr Evans, the farmer. He bent down and ran his rough hand over the stubble. His farmhand, Dai, imitated the farmer's action. 'We'll not get better than this,' he agreed. 'So shall we light up, Mr Evans?'

'Light up it is,' said Mr Evans; and threw a blazing paraffin-soaked rag on a heap of dry stalks. Red and gold flames leaped and spurted.

It didn't take long for the two of them to start a tide of fire. Driven by the wind, the fire munched its way across the stubble.

Burning off the stubble . . . Ah well, thought Mr Evans, there's an end of summer. Smoke and flames, ah well, ah well. It does the earth good. Potash and purification.

Above the field, unseen by Mr Evans and Dai, the little plane met the smoke and twitched uneasily. It fluttered like a moth, not knowing what to make of the confusion of air. It dipped, slipped, bucked, let a wing fall, lurched down-wards, tried to recover and failed. Could it have spoken, it would have said, 'No! Wait! Steady on, don't do that! Let's be reasonable!' As it was, it lapsed into a series of false starts and failures, losing height in deep swoops, gaining height only to stall and fall again.

It landed neatly enough, propped up by stubble. It still glittered and shone despite the smuts landing on it. But then the flames came closer and closer still. The plane's doped tissue wrinkled, curled, split.

A little flame jumped to a wingtip – liked what it found – and began to grow, nibbling as it grew.

SOS! HELP! SOS!
SOS! HELP
SOS!
S

Then suddenly, in a burst of flame, nothing at all.

'Yes, Gemma's all right now,' Mo told Kat. 'She's over it. Back to normal. Just leave her alone with me.' He wanted Kat out of the room. He wanted to stare out of the window again, stare until his eyes ached, stare until he felt even sicker.

'Smoke,' he said. 'Just look at it. Huge pall of smoke. And the wind—'

'You're sure the wind's blowing towards the smoke?' Gemma said.

'Don't be stupid. Of course I'm sure. If the plane meets that, she'll burn out and we've had it.'

Gemma looked at her brother's face, white with rage. At last she said, 'There's still the tunnel.'

Mo made a rude remark about what she could do to the tunnel. She shrugged, moved things aside and went to work digging. Suddenly Mo grabbed the little shovel and began digging furiously, recklessly, not caring what noise he made. Until now, the tunnel had been a downward curve, then a short level stretch. Now Mo knelt on the level and struck upwards with the shovel.

A shower of earth fell, covering him. 'Help me,' he gasped. 'Clear this muck.' He was half buried. She had to use her hands to clear round his legs and hips. All the time, he kept striking upwards, jabbing spitefully at the earth. Now the stringy roots of couch grass appeared in the soil Gemma cleared . . .

There was an even bigger fall of soil, and Mo was swamped up to his hips again. But this time it was different. This time Mo's body was bathed in light. Mo had reached the surface.

She looked out of the window and saw Mo's

head and shoulders, like some extraordinary and enormous plant that had sprouted among the weeds. His face was filthy. His hair was full of soil and bits of grass. Only his eyes looked clean.

But then he smiled and his teeth looked unnaturally clean too.

'Coo-ee,' he said, conversationally.

CHAPTER THIRTEEN

THE END OF THE TUNNEL

The escape would take place that very night. They got everything ready. Food, drink and warmth were the chief things. Their blankets would be more than good enough to supply warmth. Wine bottles would carry their water. As for food . . .

'I'm still hungry,' Gemma said humbly to Kat. 'I'm sorry, but it's always this way after one of my . . . attacks. I just have to eat and eat and eat.'

Scowling, Kat went to the kitchen. Gemma heard her throw open the bread bin and slam down the bread knife. 'Quick!' Gemma whispered over her shoulder to Mo. He made a silent, barefoot dash for the bathroom. He had to get clean: if one of the gang saw him, it would be easy to guess where all the dirt had come from. But running the taps would make a noise and Kat might hear—

'There you are,' Kat said, thrusting a plateful of bread and butter at Gemma. Bread and butter would keep them going. 'Feed your face,' said Kat.

'Oh, thank you, thank you so much, I'm sorry to trouble you, but you see when I get these attacks . . .' Gemma kept talking and talking. When Kat's back was turned, Gemma hastily wrapped the food in a magazine. As she talked, her right ear seemed to glow and grow. Above her own voice, she could hear watery sounds from the bathroom, loud sounds, deafening sounds, sounds that filled her ear. Surely Kat must hear them? Gemma dried up. Kat, one hand on a jutting hip, stared coldly at her. Gemma began blabbering again, saying anything that came into her head.

Kat cut her short. 'I've got better things to do,' she said, 'than listen to you, my fine lady. Get back to your room!'

Kat turned on her heel, snatched up her little radio and turned it on loud. So loud that if Mo had taken a high dive into the bath Kat would not have heard. Glowing with relief, Gemma got back to her room, as instructed; and showed the bread and butter to newly washed Mo, safely back from the bathroom. 'Clever old us!' Gemma said.

'Lucky old us!' Mo grinned. 'Right: back to the tunnel. Let's add the finishing touches!'

*

The tunnel was ready. It was even lined. As Gemma said, 'We don't want to *look* like escapees, all filthy and rotten, when we reach some house or other and ask for help.' So they laid plastic sacks on the floor and sides of the tunnel.

'Staying awake,' Mo said. 'We'll do an hour each. I'll go first. At three in the morning, we take off, OK? And don't fall asleep when it's your turn. Don't eat too much dinner, it will make you sleepy. And don't—'

Gemma gave him her dead-fish look and he stopped; then laughed. 'Just think, Gem,' he said, 'five hours from now, we'll be on our way. And twelve hours from now, we'll be headline news. PLUCKY CHILDREN MAKE FREEDOM DASH. BOY HERO SAVES SOBBING SISTER.'

Gemma said, 'GIRL HEROINE'S COURAGE SAVES USELESS BROTHER!' and got Mo in a headlock.

They wrestled vaguely for a minute or two but their hearts were not in it. Escape! That was what mattered.

At ten, they were sent to bed by a surly Kat. They lay awake, talking in undertones, till twelve.

At twelve, Mo said, 'Sleep, Gem', and he

stayed awake. At one she took over, holding his luminous wristwatch and staring at it determinedly. She woke him at two and managed to sleep, though her excitement made her heart thump.

At three, she heard him say, 'Gem! Gem!' and was angry with him for pulling at her shoulder. But then she remembered and was wide awake. Without a word, they silently cleared the mouth of the tunnel and picked up their burdens. Mo was ready first. He looked out of the window. Perfect. A bright but not moonlit sky. No rain or sign of rain. Not cold. And silence: nothing and no one stirring.

'OK, Gem?'

'OK. We're going?'

'Yep. Ladies first.'

She lowered herself into the tunnel and reached out her hands for her blanket bundle. As he began to hand it to her, he heard a distant droning sound.

'*Car*,' he said.

'Doesn't matter,' she whispered back. 'Hand me my stuff. Come on—'

'No, wait. It's coming closer.'

'Who cares? Give me my stuff—'

'No, *wait!*'

The car was very near now. Much too near. Surely it couldn't be coming to the farm? But

Mo and Gemma heard the familiar *rang-a-dang-a-dang* as the car crossed the cattle grid: and now the car's lights were illuminating walls and trees . . .

Then voices and movements. Kat, cross and sleepy, calling 'Michael's here, Macko. Where's Per?'

'Yeah, I'm up . . . Where's Per?'

Frantically, Gemma and Mo put the bed back over the tunnel mouth and got the room back to normal.

Kat's voice again. 'The kids, Macko. Kick their backsides and get them out here.'

Footsteps; and Macko's huge body filling the doorway, blocking out the light, and his voice saying, 'Yeah, well, come on you two, don't mess about, just toothbrushes and things, come *on*. We're leaving. Moving house.'

Then they were bumping along again in the camper van with Michael, Per, Kat and Macko.

Back where they started from. Back to Square One.

CHAPTER FOURTEEN

PUFFER

The camper van went on and on through the night. Michael drove. He seemed tireless. Kat, Per and Macko dozed now and then. Gemma slept, fitfully and crossly. She leaned heavily against Mo at first, her sharp elbows digging into him when she twitched.

He could not sleep. He stared out through the windows into the moving darkness that trundled past the windows and thought of the tunnel – useless and deserted – and the plane, on which he had wasted so much energy. He could see every detail of it in his mind's eye.

Gemma's elbow dug at him. He dug back at her crossly. She woke. 'You might let me *sleep*,' she said, unreasonably. 'You keep *moving*.' Mo snorted. Gemma got up, stretched, blinked, yawned – and fell sideways as the camper van went round the corner. She landed on Per's lap. 'You'll do,' she said, indistinctly, and burrowed into him as if he were a bed, falling asleep instantly. Per looked noble and frowning and let her sleep. He even put an arm round her. Mo glared at his sister, wishing his eyes were death rays. In fact, they were merely large things in his skull that felt as if they had been rolled in pepper.

'Where are we going? When do we *get* there?' he asked Macko for the tenth time. Macko, for the tenth time, made no answer.

A Police car, a small Ford, was on patrol that night. It usually had a crew of two, PCs Mavis Ronaldson and Don Stewart. For the past two nights, the little car had to use all its power because of a third man, a big, heavy man, PC Blowers. 'Bet they call you Puffer!' Mavis said when they first met. 'That's right,' the big man said, grinning sheepishly.

He always appeared sheepish. Not shy-sheepish but woolly-sheepish. It was a physical thing. His curly, tawny hair made you think of a wool. His body and face, though not fat, had a sheep-like fullness. His manner was pleasant, restful and sheepish.

'Anything particular?' Don Stewart asked, that first night. He meant, 'Have you been sent to join us for any particular reason?'

'No,' said PC Blowers. 'Just here for the ride . . . get to know the district, you know the sort of thing.' Mavis and Don nodded. They knew the sort of thing very well. Orders from above: don't ask questions, just obey.

For two nights, they drove and Puffer just sat. He was easy company. Tonight he suddenly said, 'That camper van!'

'What about it?'

'Hang on to it.'

So Mavis, who was driving, followed the camper van that had just gone by. It was doing a steady 40 mph to begin with, but then its speed went up to 50. 'What's interesting about it?' Mavis said over her shoulder. Puffer said, 'Don't know yet. Probably nothing. But that Embassy kidnapping, you remember – they took off in a camper van.'

Mavis said, 'Ah! But that was a week ago, wasn't it?' To the camper van, she said, 'Steady, friend! You're not built for it!' For now the camper van was up in the mid-fifties and lurching uneasily on corners.

'Get closer,' Puffer said. 'Want a look-see inside.'

'Have to overtake to see,' Mavis said. 'That suit you?'

'Fine, overtake.'

Mavis put her foot down. When she was level with the camper van, she switched the lights to main beam to give her passengers a better view. 'At least four of them,' Don said. 'And two of them are kids!'

'Good for you, Puffer,' Mavis said. 'We could have something here.'

As she spoke, the camper van jerked its rear end as the driver made a bad gear change: and took off. Its driver was not going to be overtaken. 'Hell!' said Mavis, as the big vehicle lurched and swung. She braked to let it get ahead then tucked in behind. 'Not too close!' Don warned, as the camper van, bucketing and bouncing, tried to go still faster. 'You don't have to tell me!' Mavis said. She looked grim. 'Driving like that with *kids* . . .' she muttered.

The road widened. The camper van driver gave up. He pulled to the curb and halted. Without a word Don went to the driver's window, Mavis to the other side and Puffer to the back door.

The driver's door slid back and the driver jumped out. He stood facing Don. 'Police! I didn't know you were Police!' he said, his voice high with anger and fear. 'How was I to know? You *made* me break the speed limit, following us like that!—'

'As you say, sir,' Don replied, without listening. 'Mind if I take a look inside?'

'Supposing *I* mind?' shouted a girl's voice. She tumbled out, angry. Her hair was cropped short and dyed green and purple. She was small. 'Provocation!' she shouted. 'Pigs! Victimization!'

'As you say, miss,' Don said and shone his torch into the camper van.

'Doing a gig, we were,' said the young man. 'We got aggro enough there without you lot victimizing us!—'

The head of another girl rose from among the guitar cases, amplifiers and lighting systems. This girl's face was like a panda's, with great black patches grease-painted over the eyes. She, too, was very small. 'We've had trouble enough without *you!*' she shouted. 'Look what they did to our gear!' She pointed at a combo amp. The grille had been kicked in. But you could still read the group's name: SLIPPED DISCO.

'Slipped Disco,' Puffer said, mildly. 'Nice little group. My daughter's one of your fans. Shall we go, Don?'

You made me break the speed limit!' shouted the driver. 'Pigs!' screamed the girl with the green and purple hair. 'Aggro, nothing but aggro!' moaned the girl with the panda face. The fourth man in the camper van appeared from behind a pile of gear and patted her back. 'You charging us with something?' he demanded of Don.

'No question of that, sir,' said Don. 'Routine check, nothing but routine.'

'Very nice group, yours,' Puffer said.

'Drive carefully,' smiled Mavis.

They got back in their Ford and Mavis engaged first gear.

Don chuckled. 'Slipped Disco . . . Long way from your Embassy kidnapping, Puffer! And we'd even got the kids wrong. Those two girls weren't exactly kids.' 'Natural mistake,' Puffer said. 'Those short haircuts. And women have smaller skulls than men.'

'But bigger brains,' Mavis said. 'Embassy kidnapping . . . I'll give you Embassy kidnapping!'

Skilfully and cheerfully, she steered round a hedgehog that was gravely crossing the road. 'Dawn,' she said. The sky was beginning to light up. 'Another two hours or so and we're off duty . . .'

CHAPTER FIFTEEN

TRUCE

'Dawn,' Mo muttered. The sky was a dirty grey and rain fell out of it ceaselessly. He tried to remember how to swear in German, but could not recall the words. Not being able to swear made him feel like swearing.

Kat was awake and rattling tea things in the back of the camper van. Good. The noise meant a hot drink. The other sleepers were wakened by the clattering. They rubbed their eyes and looked tousled and ridiculous.

Per got up. First he had to lift and lower Gemma. He carefully re-arranged her so that she lay on the seat, asleep. The camper van lurched, however, and she woke, sat up, spoke. 'Are you going away?' she said foggily to Per. 'I wish you wouldn't.' Peevishly, she tried to re-settle herself. Per smiled and moved away.

Kat saw and overheard. Her face darkened. 'Now look what you've done!' she said harshly to Per. 'Disturbed the fairy princess! The sleeping beauty!' She threw teaspoons into mugs, accurately and noisily. Per, confused, said 'Please? What do you wish?'

'Oh never mind my wishes,' Kat said. '*I'm* not anyone special. *I'm* no fairy princess!'

'You can say that again,' Macko guffawed.

Kat held a saucepan of near-boiling water in her hand. For a moment it looked as if she might throw it at Macko. She did not. Her straight spine tensed, her dark face lowered and hid itself from him, her firm hand poured water into the mugs. Once, her hand let her down and some water spilled. But only once.

Gemma, properly awake now, felt a surprising emotional sympathy for Kat. She was actually sorry, she realized, for leather-handed, slap-happy Kat! Now she was Krumpled Kat; Kat with Per's indifferent back and Macko's jeering face turned to her.

There was a plastic bag of runner beans in a corner. Kat had picked them at the farm. Gemma said, 'Those beans, Kat—'

'Well, what about them?'

'Shall I string and slice them?'

Kat shrugged and chucked Gemma a little kitchen knife. Gemma got to work on the beans. Kat shouted 'Coffee, tea. Come and get it. Put your own milk and sugar in.' Because there was nowhere else to sit, Kat sat down next to Gemma.

Her face was set. She seemed to radiate waves of bottled-up energy. Gemma felt the waves. 'Am I doing the beans right?' she offered. Again Kat shrugged. 'Who cares?' she seemed to say.

But she could not resist glancing sideways at Gemma's work. What she saw displeased her. 'String them both sides,' she said. 'And don't cut them so small.' She got another knife and joined Gemma in the bean-slicing. She worked three times faster than Gemma. Bits of beans seemed to spray from her hands.

Gemma tried another offering of words. 'Gosh, you're quick!' she said. 'You're so good at things,' she added.

'Oh yeah, I'm good, I'm terrific, I'm the great-est,' Kat said tonelessly and then, somehow, over the noise of the rain and the camper van's engine, they were talking to each other. Talking in low, unhurried voices, as friends talk. And somehow, the talk got round to the Cause.

'I suppose I'm always . . . *angry*,' Kat said. 'Anger's a sort of habit with me now. I haven't travelled as much as you, but I've seen more. You've been there, but I've *been there*. I've seen . . . things they wouldn't let you see. I mean, you're a kid. Famines, I've seen famines. I've been *involved* with starving people. Trying to help them. Relief work. I've driven a lorry with sacks of mouldy rice in the back, and people begging by the roadside, putting their hands out for muck that *you* wouldn't eat in a million years.'

'But that's not my fault,' Gemma began.

'I know, I didn't mean that . . . It's not your fault and it's not your business. You're just a kid, a privileged kid. Not that I'm accusing you, although I suppose I am . . . But I've been there, India, Laos, all kinds of places. And it was my business, I had to do something, anything.'

'And that's the Cause?' Gemma suggested. Kat did not need to answer.

Gemma wanted an answer. 'The cause that people like Michael and you and Per are fighting for?' she said. As she spoke, she realized her mistake.

'Per?' Kat flared. 'Who's talking about Per? Or the others? Per, always Per . . . Those *beans*: you're supposed to string them first, slice them after!' she spat. She held up a sliced bean with a curl of string hanging from it. 'You stupid little cow,' she said. 'Can't you even slice beans?'

Mo jerked his head up, listening. He watched Kat glare at Gemma – watched Gemma's eyes recover from the shock, then become hard. He watched as Gemma, insultingly dainty, took the bit of bean from Kat's fingers and peeled away the offending dangle of string. 'Silly little me!'

Gemma mewed, keeping her eyes fixed on Kat's. 'Stupid little cow!' she lisped. The words could be taken either way.

And then of course Kat hit Gemma and Gemma kept staring into Kat's eyes.

Truce over, Mo thought. Back to business as usual.

CHAPTER SIXTEEN

THE GARAGE

T he camper van's engine and exhaust roared and echoed and the light outside the windows darkened. End of the journey, thought Mo. We're in an enclosed place. 'Everyone out,' Michael said. He sounded tired. They all got out.

'Our new home,' Gemma said, looking about her. '*Charming!*'

They were in a deserted garage. Any garage, Mo thought, in any town, anywhere. A big, ugly, old, cold, empty, deserted garage. He could hear traffic but it was a long way away. There were no neighbourly noises. A telephone? He could not see one, not even in the glass-walled booth in the corner, the place marked Office. All that remained of the garage's busy days were posters – Shell, Champion, Dunlop, the usual signs: but all grey and old.

There was a pin-up calendar, though. He edged towards it to read the date. 1977. Oh Lord,

Mo thought, that was a long time ago. The gang have chosen a good hideout.

He and Gemma were taken upstairs. It had been some sort of flat where people lived. There were still greasy stains on the wall where someone had fried food on a small cooker. Their room's door had an outside Yale lock, a lock Mo knew he couldn't pick. Kat and Macko threw sleeping-bags at them. 'Get yourselves organized,' Kat commanded. 'You're going to be here a nice long time.'

Gemma, nose-in-the-air and ready for a fight, said, 'Why a long time? Can't you get the money for us? No lovely lolly? Aren't you even going to get a mangy fur coat for kidnapping us! Poor old you!'

Kat moved forward, hand raised ready for slapping. Mo suddenly furious, shouted, 'Leave my sister alone!' He felt his face go scarlet with instant rage and enjoyed the feeling. Macko said 'Cut it out, Kat, save it for later.' As he spoke he rolled his eyes at Mo and Gemma as if to say, 'Take no notice of her'. Kat sullenly turned away. She and Macko clattered down the bare creaking stairs, locking the door on the captives.

Gemma and Mo exchanged glances. Mo said. 'See! They're beginning to crumble at the edges.

Quarrelling. Bad tempers. They're sick of it all. It's gone on too long for them.'

Gemma said, 'It's gone on too long for us, too!'

'Yes, but it's more serious for them, don't you see? They're all twitchy, they're not properly in charge any more.'

'So what do we do?' Gemma said.

'Divide and conquer! Pit one against the other! Get them quarrelling!'

'Divide and conquer . . .' Gemma mused.

Mo seized her arm and said, 'Divide and conquer *them*, Gemma. Not *us*. We've got to stick together'.

'What do you mean?'

'I mean you and your pash on Per, Gem!'

'I haven't got a pash on him! Leave go my arm!'

'You have.'

'I haven't.'

It was like being little children again. Mo said, 'Cross your heart and hope to die and say, "I haven't got a pash on Per". Go on, say it!'

She giggled and broke free. He chased her and caught her. But he never did get her to say what he wanted her to say.

CHAPTER SEVENTEEN

D & C

D & C, Dividing and Conquering, was easier than they had thought possible. It was also enjoyable.

'Do big muscles really mean great strength?' Gemma innocently asked Macko.

He smirked. 'Want me to prove it?' he said, and picked her up with one hand, gripping her under her armpit. Gemma squealed delightedly. 'Oh, you really *are* strong!' she cried girlishly. 'Isn't he strong, Kat?' Kat growled and turned away. She hated Macko, of course; she had never forgiven him for beating her up that day in the field outside the farmhouse.

'Do you think he could lift *you*, Kat?' Gemma, knowing very well what would – and did – happen. 'What, lift *her*?' Macko said. 'What, me lay hands on Kat? You've got to be joking!' He roared with laughter at his own wit. Kat glowered.

Leaving Kat and Macko to their long, bitter

quarrel, Mo and Gemma went to their room and planned the next instalment.

It began with Gemma, looking very young and piteous, saying, 'I know you don't like me, Kat. I know you think I'm Per's "fairy princess" and all that—'

Kat slammed tea things about on a dirty table.

'But you're all wrong, absolutely wrong!' Gemma said, looking up at Kat with huge dark eyes filled with tears and sincerity. 'There's only one person Per cares about,' Gemma continued. Kat pretended not to listen. 'One special person,' Gemma said in a hushed voice. 'Guess who . . .'

Kat, her face very hot, said, 'Get out of my way, you little—'

'Guess who,' Gemma repeated, softly.

'Don't waste my time,' Kat said, doing violent things to a kettle.

'*You!*' Gemma said, thrillingly.

Later, she told Per that Kat was mad about him – always had been, always would be. Per looked deeply embarrassed, as Mo and Gemma knew he would. From then on, he avoided speaking to Kat or even looking at her; and this neglect made Kat all the more miserable, bad-tempered, distracted and quarrelsome.

'It also makes her an inefficient kidnapper,' Mo happily reminded Gemma.

Michael was an easy subject for D and C; easy, because always worried. Mo and Gemma simply gave him more to worry about.

Mo and Gemma spent hours peering out of their grimy little window at the bleak view. There was the distant, constantly busy major road (only the tops of the cars and lorries could be seen); and nearby, the puddled, cracked ribbon of service road, always deserted.

They filled it with imaginary vehicles. 'Oh, look!' Gemma might say, pointing at a bored sparrow. 'There's Princess Diana on her moped!' And so on and so on.

Now they invented a mysterious car with which to worry Michael.

'We saw the car again,' Mo began. Michael swallowed the bait. 'What car? Where? When?' he said.

'Oh, the usual one,' Gemma said. 'The Honda with three men in it.'

'Rover,' Mo corrected her.

Michael said, 'Never mind that, *when* did you see it? What was it doing?'

'Oh, it just parked,' Gemma said, airily. 'And the men ate sandwiches.'

'Same as yesterday,' Mo said. 'Three men, all eating things. One had a camera, or something—'

Michael's face went a strange colour. He got up and hurried out. Mo and Gemma heard voices in the next room, voices getting louder and more worried. Then Michael came back with Per and the two of them grilled Mo and Gemma about the car, Per frowning deeply and Michael constantly taking off his glasses and putting them on again.

'They're worried stiff,' Mo said happily, when he was alone with Gemma.

'Worried stiff!' Gemma agreed. 'Nice, wasn't it? I enjoyed it. I'm a good liar.'

'I'd enjoy it more if there really had been a car,' Mo said. 'I'm sick of being kidnapped. I wish our rescue really would start . . .'

CHAPTER EIGHTEEN

THE RESCUER

M o's wish came true. A rescuer arrived that very night.

Mo was woken by sounds from downstairs; creakings, scrabblings, secret noises. 'Rats!' Mo whispered, and sat up in bed, his heart pounding. He feared rats. He looked at Gemma. She was deeply asleep.

'Not rats,' he murmured, a minute later. There was a purpose behind the noises. They were regular. Woodwork creaked and strained.

Someone was trying to force a way in.

Then another noise, much more frightening: someone in the next room – almost certainly Macko – was getting out of bed very cautiously and silently. Squeaking bed-springs, creaking floorboards. Tip-toeing footsteps in the corridor. A muttered conversation as Macko, if it was Macko, woke Per.

A metallic click just outside the bedroom door. Per's voice whispering, 'You are not to shoot, you understand?' And Macko's grunted reply.

Mo crept out of bed, not knowing what to do. Warn the intruder? Suppose the intruder was not the rescuer, but just a thief, a tramp?

The question was settled for him by a tearing noise downstairs as timber gave way – the crash of a falling door – shouts, breaking glass, yells – Kat running down the stairs – Gemma, awake and terrified, shouting, 'What's *happening!*' – distant thuds and thumps and a cry of pain – the sound of a heavy body falling . . .

A brief silence; then footsteps coming upstairs. It was Kat. She flung open the door and said, 'You two. Downstairs. Quick.'

One small electric light bulb showed Gemma and Mo all they needed to know. Per held his revolver pointed at a big man lying bleeding on the floor. Michael, professorish in pyjamas, stared at the man and nervously adjusted his spectacles. Macko, triumphant, grinned and massaged his knuckles.

The man on the floor groaned and moved. Macko kicked him, not hard, grinned and said, 'All right, friend. Name, rank and number. That's the form, isn't it? Let's hear you.' He waved his revolver and kicked the man again.

The man's nose was bloody and his face blotched where Macko had hit him. 'Got kids

of my own,' he said, indistinctly. 'Filthy lot . . .
kidnapping . . .'

'*Ah!*' Macko said, nodding significantly at Per
and Michael. 'So you're the one-man liberation
army, right? Tell us more, friend. Tell us everything. Name first.'

'Blowers,' said the man. 'PC Blowers.'

'Police Constable Blowers,' Macko said.
'Always pleased to meet a member of the Force,
I'm sure. Here on official business, are you? More
of you outside?'

PC Blowers said, 'Give me a handkerchief or
something . . . No, just on my own. Unofficial.'

Kat handed him a rag. He wiped away blood
and sat up. He was big, heavy, perhaps even
powerful; but beside Macko, with his hard
muscles bulging through the track suit he slept
in, PC Blowers looked innocent, almost childish.

'Got kids of your own, is that it?' Macko grinned. 'Thought you'd rescue these little darlings
here, did you?'

PC Blowers said, 'Wish I could have done . . .
harming kids . . .' Macko laughed jeeringly.

'Can I get him some water or something?'
Gemma said, chokingly.

Kat said, 'I'll see to that. Get out, you two.
Back to bed. And no chat.'

They obeyed her by going to bed, but they

talked. 'What about that man, that PC Blowers?' Mo whispered.

'His poor face . . .' Gemma whispered back. 'Macko really worked him over. Wonder what they'll do with him now?'

'Nothing,' Mo said. 'Just add him to the collection. Us and him. He's useless. He won't try anything now, not after what Macko did to him. Hey, the door's not locked! Shall we creep out and see what's happening?'

'You can,' Gemma said in a small voice. 'I don't want to. His poor face . . .'

He crept out and down the stairs. The gang were talking in the kitchen, out of sight. The only person Mo saw was PC Blowers. He was all alone in a separate bay of the garage, a sort of cell. He sat hunched up, bound by thick, rubbery electric cable round his wrists and neck. If he tried to move he would strangle himself. His face looked worse than ever.

As Mo, unseen, watched, PC Blowers did something completely mad. First, he kicked off his shoes, one by one. Then he let himself fall sideways, grunting with pain as the cables tugged and cut into him. Finally, he shuffled himself into a position where his face almost touched his shoes: *and began talking.* Talking to his shoes!

The absurd conversation lasted perhaps a

minute. Mo was so astonished that he half stood. Puffer saw him. He jerked his head as if to say, 'Come over here.' Mo obeyed. 'Do you want me to undo you?' he whispered.

'No! Just my shoes! Put them on again!'

'What do you mean? If I undo you, you can escape—'

'Put my shoes on! Quick! And lace them up properly! Hurry!'

'But—'

'Put them *on!*'

Concussion, Mo thought. One blow too many on the head. He untied the laces, put on the shoes and tied the laces again.

'Don't tell anyone, get it?' PC Blowers said hoarsely. Obviously he was ashamed of himself.

'But I can undo this stuff – set you free!—'

'Never mind about that. Now *go!*'

Mo returned to his bed. Gemma was waiting. 'Well?' she said.

'He seems OK,' Mo mumbled.

'What's he *doing*?'

'Nothing. Just – recovering,' Mo lied.

What was the point of telling Gemma the absurd truth? – that the poor man had been talking, talking to his *shoes!*

CHAPTER NINETEEN

THE TAPE RECORDER

The kidnappers were losing heart. There was no doubt about it. And they were growing careless.

At first, they had forbidden Mo and Gemma even to speak to PC Blowers. Now, they and everyone else spoke with him: Macko to jeer at him, Per to question him, Michael to probe into his history and background. They kept him bound and separated, yet allowed Mo and Gemma to be near him.

Gemma became his faithful nurse. She fed him, shaved him, tended his wounds and insisted loudly that he be taken to the lavatory at regular times. She learned his nickname, Puffer, and called him by it.

She treated him like a pet animal. He behaved like one. He was mildly grateful to her for everything she did; mildly curious about Macko's great strength ('I thought I'd met some tough ones in my time, but *you* . . .!'); mildly happy when his bonds were loosened and he was allowed to walk about for five minutes, with Macko's gun following every step; mildly obedient when Macko said, 'Right, time's up. Down on your knees, then, let's tie you up again, nice . . . and . . . neat!'

'If only he'd argue or complain or fight back in some way!' Gemma complained to Mo. 'It's – it's humiliating, even to watch him! Like a dumb animal!'

Mo said, 'I'm afraid that's all he is. A sort of human baa-lamb. Not much of a rescuer, Gem.'

She sighed and bullied Kat into giving her a piece of cloth to fold into a pad for Puffer's neck. The cable was rubbing a raw, red line round his throat.

Michael came in, walking with a lively step. His eyes glinted behind his glasses. 'Well, it's almost all over,' he announced. 'Listen!' He put the little tape recorder on the table and started it. 'You kids can listen too,' he told Mo and Gemma.

The tape recorder said its piece. They heard Michael's and other voices. Michael repeated his demands: the other voices agreed. The talk went on for a long time, but it came down to an official voice telling Michael, 'All right then. One million pounds. And a getaway car, as you say. With safe conduct.'

'What about PC Blowers?' said Michael's voice.

'Well, that's a separate matter. We're interested in the children. PC Blowers doesn't come into it, surely? You merely release him in your own time at your own discretion.'

Michael stopped the tape and grinned. Per said, 'This is very good, I think. And the times and dates?'

'Whenever you say, Per. The later we set them, the better. Everything last-minute. Less chance for them to try any fun and games.'

'Fun and games? Oh, yes I understand. Again, you are right. Deliver at the last minute.'

'When?' Mo interrupted.

'Quite soon now,' Per told him. 'Very soon indeed. It is nearly over now. That is good.'

'Good enough to drink to!' Macko said. 'Come on, everyone! Let's open a bottle!'

They went to the kitchen.

Mo stole the tape recorder.

CHAPTER TWENTY

GUN PLAY

I n the kitchen, the kidnappers' party started
well then turned sour. Mo and Gemma, left
alone, listened to everything. Gemma even put
her ear against the door. 'Macko's clowning
about!' she reported. 'And he's drinking like
crazy!' Mo pretended not to be interested.

'Look, never mind about them,' he said. 'What
about us? Why don't we sneak out—'

'All the doors are locked, stupid.'

'But if I untied PC Blowers—'

'Oh him! The baa-lamb! Fat lot of good he'd
be. Macko's taking his umpteenth drink. Ooops!'
There were footsteps on the other side of the
door. Gemma ran to the table and sat innocently
tearing a piece of bread. Kat came in, her face
cross and suspicious.

'You two behaving yourselves?' she said.

'Oh, *yes!*' Gemma smirked. 'We're behaving
ever so nicely, thank you!' She gave Kat a butter-
wouldn't-melt-in-my-mouth look, then turned
her head to stare through the open door. Through

it, she could see Michael, grinning uncertainly as he poured a can of beer down his throat; Per drinking as if the drink were poison; and Macko. Already Macko was red and sweating and noisy. 'Watch this, then!' he bellowed. 'Look at me, Per! Look, Michael! I balance this glass of beer on my forehead, get it? – then I bend backwards, like this . . .'

The trick went wrong. The glass toppled, beer flowed over Macko's face and chest. He gaped and grinned and roared and mopped at himself. 'No, hang on!' he shouted. 'It's a great trick, you got to see it! Now watch, just you watch!'

'Yes, we're behaving ever so nicely,' Gemma repeated, giving Kat her sweetest smile. 'And you – are you lot behaving nicely in there?'

Macko's glass fell and smashed on the floor. Kat's open palm fell and smashed on Gemma's face. 'Don't try getting clever with me!' Kat choked, raising her hand again. Gemma ducked. The slap landed on the side of her head with sufficient force to knock her off her chair.

Mo would have gone to Gemma's rescue quicker than he did but for the cassette recorder. He had to get rid of it first. He put it on the floor and gently kicked it towards the darkness under the centre of the table. This done, he ran at Kat. He hit her in the stomach with his fist.

As the punch went in, he thought how hard her stomach was. Hard and springy, tight with bunched muscle. 'Tough!' he just had time to think – and then she became a sort of mobile, flailing blur, advancing on him, pushing him back with slap after slap on his face and head, dazzling him, hurting him. To make things worse, there was a voice in the back of his head. 'No gentleman,' it said primly, 'ever raises his hand to strike a woman!' The voice, the memory, confused him. As the slaps rained down, he tried to remember where it came from. Berlin, that was it, when he was four or five or something, and they had an English nanny. 'No gentleman ever raises his hand—'

And suddenly Macko was there, grinning and roaring, confusing him still more. 'That's right, lovely!' he shouted, being a boxing commentator. 'Nice left and right to the head, that's the way, she's throwing punches from all angles! And our boy's on the ropes, trying to cover up, only the bell can save him now!' He must have hit the sugar bowl with a spoon, for Mo heard the sharp *ping*! Then he was lifted effortlessly and plonked down in a chair and Macko was standing over him, flapping at his face with a napkin. 'The big question now, folks,' Macko shouted, 'is – can our boy come out for the next round?'

102

Kat still loomed over him, ready to hit him, but Macko kept her at bay simply by stretching out his enormous hand. 'No, stand back there, fair's fair!' he shouted. 'He's thrown in the towel!' The napkin fluttered into Kat's face. 'Want to say a few words into the mike, boyo? Tell us why you lost?' Macko continued, delighted with himself. Gemma, tear-stained and furious, snatched a salt cellar and threw it at Macko. It missed him and smashed against the door frame, covering Per and Michael, just entering, with salt and broken glass.

'You should not do that, I think!' Per said.

'Cut it out!' Michael shouted, his voice high and nervous.

'That's telling 'em!' Macko bellowed, still delighted with himself. 'Cool it! Everybody freeze!' He flourished his revolver. 'If it's the last thing I do, you coyotes,' he said, pretending to be the Sheriff of a Western town, 'I'll bring law and order to this township!'

He spun the gun round his finger. It glinted and flickered. His index finger was so big that he had to use his little finger to spin the gun.

'Macko, you stop now!' Per warned. He was too late. The gun escaped. It spun over the table, bounced into a corner and went off with an enormous bang. The smoke billowed delicately from the corner. Macko looked at it with puzzled surprise. The smoke cleared and everyone could see a small blackened hole where the bullet had entered the wall.

'I didn't mean—' Macko begin.

'You stupid great oaf,' Kat said.

'Someone could have been killed!' Michael said indignantly.

Macko said 'Well, I mean, it was an accident. No harm done.' Awkwardly, he recovered his gun from the corner. 'I filed the sear a bit,' he explained, 'to make the trigger lighter, know what I mean? Perhaps I overdid it . . . It shouldn't have gone off like that, of its own accord . . .' He shook his head at the gun, as if it had been naughty.

'Give it to me,' Per said, stretching out his hand.

'My gun? Give it to you?'

'I am asking you, give me the gun. Quickly, now.'

For a moment it looked as if Macko might obey. He made an uncertain movement with his hand, almost offering the gun – then snatched it back again.

'You got to be joking!' he said. 'It's *my* gun!' He stuck out his jaw. 'You want it,' he said, 'you come and take it! Come on then!'

He stood there, huge and untrustworthy, simple and dangerous. Per moved towards him, hand outstretched. Macko did not give ground. He stared at Per with round, puzzled but unafraid eyes. The fingers of his hand clenched the butt of the gun; his biceps muscles swelled and bunched. '*My* gun,' he said.

Still Per moved forward. His face too was set, determined – yet slightly puzzled. The gun no longer mattered: it was the battle of wills that counted. 'You give me!' Per said in a very low voice – and jerked his cupped hand forward.

Then Gemma was between the two of them. 'Stop it! Don't!' she cried. She clasped her arms round Per's waist. 'He'll hurt you! Don't! It's silly!' She tried to push Per back with her thin arms. 'Please!' she said. 'He'll hurt you!'

And suddenly it was all over. Kat sniffed and scowled, Michael fiddled with his spectacles, Per said 'But I do not like guns, they are bad things', and Macko gave a grunting laugh, scornful but not too loud. He kept his gun.

Now he seemed at ease. He sat at the table, shoulders spread, massive arms and hands busy. He stripped the gun with a great show of expertise; jerked the bullets from the chamber; and ranged them neatly in a semicircle. 'Got to clean it,' he told Mo, in a mild, friendly voice. 'Always clean the bore after firing or you get corrosion. Corrosion, that's what you get. Did you know that?'

Embarrassed, Per, Kat and Michael left the room. Kat seized Gemma by the crook of her arm and jerked her away, saying 'All right, young lady, you can do the vegetables. *Now.*' Mo was alone with Macko.

Mo said nothing. He was thinking of two things: the cassette recorder under the table and the square bulge in the back pocket of Macko's jeans. The first had to be hidden. The second had to be revealed.

'Bet you've got lots of bullets!' he said at last.

'Cartridges, not bullets,' Macko corrected him.

'Well, I bet you've got lots.'

Macko winked, looked wise and patted the square bulge in his back pocket. 'I got enough,' he replied. 'I mean, what's the good of a gun without ammo? Right?' He winked at Mo.

'Right!' Mo replied and winked back. He made his face wondering and boyish and said 'Real cartridges! I wouldn't mind a look at them! Go on, Macko, be a sport. Let's have a look!'

'You got to be joking,' Macko replied. He swelled his chest importantly.

'No, seriously; just a look. Go on, Macko.

There's nobody here. Per's in the other room, *he* can't see!'

'*Per*?' Macko said. 'What do you mean, *Per*? Who cares about him?'

'I know you don't!' Mo said, in a tone of humble admiration. 'You know how to handle him . . .'

Mo kept up the pressure: and won. At last, the worn little cardboard box was fished from the back pocket. At last Mo was able to hold it, open it and poke his fingers at the cartridges. He made wondering noises and faces.

Then, inevitably, he dropped the box and the cartridges scattered on the floor.

Naturally, he picked them all up and replaced them in the box, every single one of them – except for the four he managed to hide behind the already hidden cassette recorder.

'There's some missing!' Macko grumbled, when the cardboard lid was replaced. 'The box feels lighter.'

'They're all there, honest!' Mo said. 'Go on, count them. How many did you have?'

'How should I know?' Macko complained, telling Mo exactly what he wanted to know. 'I mean, these are just the ones I carry for reloading. I don't count them. I just grab a handful—'

'Well, that's all right, then, isn't it?' Mo said.

Macko looked uncertain but eventually nodded. Later, he went to get a beer. Mo, alone, threw a napkin under the table; went to pick it up; and used it to conceal the cassette recorder. He put the cartridges in his pocket. They felt smooth and weighty.

Upstairs, Gemma was already asleep. Quietly, Mo concealed his treasures. All but one of the cartridges went under a loose floorboard – a small piece of loose wood that no one could ever possibly discover. The cassette recorder was tucked into an airbrick near the ceiling. Mo had to stand on his bed to reach up to it. 'Clever!' he muttered, as the little machine slid out of sight. He smiled.

CHAPTER TWENTY-ONE

LITTLE CHUM

He smiled because he was thinking about his gun.

He had a gun. A real one. He'd made it himself. He called it Little Chum. He did not know or care where the name came from; it wasn't an original name, he'd read it somewhere. But the gun was highly original.

It began when he found a piece of high-quality steel tube, about seven inches long and chromium-plated. He had held it over his fist and pointed it at Gemma. 'See this rod, sister? It means curtains for you!'

She took her part in the old joke. 'Why's that?' she said, fluttering her eyelashes.

'Because it's a curtain rod!'

'Ha, ha. Tee hee. Ho ho,' Gemma said, obediently. Then she said 'Macko and his gun . . . If only we had a gun! Then he wouldn't be Mr Tough Guy.'

Mo looked at her. His eyes had widened. He went to work.

He began by asking himself, What is a gun?

A tube, a spout for the bullet to go through. Another tube, shorter and stouter than the first tube, strong enough to hold the explosion of the cartridge.

And to make the cartridge explode, a hammer with a firing pin sticking out of it, like the point of a nail. The hammer and its firing pin had to be flung forward, fast. The pin hit the percussion cap in the base of the cartridge and – and that was it. No need for proper triggers and actions: all he needed was a hefty spring fastened to the hammer, which could be held back in the crook of his thumb against the pressure of the spring. Let it go and – bang! – the gun would fire.

He collected bits of scrap metal. There were plenty of oddments in the garage. Soon he had so many that he had to sit down with them and sort them out, fitting one bit to another. He found the short, fat, strong tube he needed almost at once. The chromium-plated tube was, luckily, a tight push-fit. He had to hammer the two bits together. He made as much noise as possible, deciding that if anyone became curious, he could say, 'I'm just hitting things, because I *feel* like it.'

The block of metal for the hammer and firing pin – and the spring that had to be firmly fastened to the hammer – took longer. But at last he found the right parts – springs from an old car distributor, a slug of metal that was just a slug of metal but happened to be right because it had been hacksawed. A slot ran down it. The springs could be jammed in the slot.

The most delicate part, the firing pin, must have come to him straight from heaven. It was unbelievable luck. The slug of metal that had been hacksawed had also been spun in a lathe. The person doing it must have thrown it aside and started afresh – for there was a little nipple, a point, sticking out of the centre of the slug. A ready-made firing pin.

He squatted in a dirty, dusty corner and drew his gun. It looked like this.

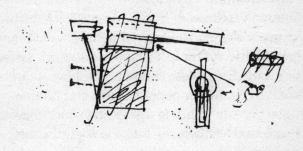

The handle was a block of wood. Metal clips from an electrical conduit held the gun together. Twists of wire ensured that it would hold together. He frowned at his drawings, changed this and that, nodded and got on with the thing that mattered, the gun itself, Little Chum. Assembling it took a surprisingly short time. Holding it, so solid and cold and chunky, gave him a thrill he had to share. He showed it to Gemma.

'Terrific!' she said. 'Brilliant! Even if it doesn't work—'

'It will work, I keep telling you. I'm not fooling around, this is a gun, it fires bullets.'

'Do you really mean it?' Gemma said, in a changed voice. 'You do, don't you? With that and a bullet—'

'I've got cartridges,' Mo said. 'And I've got a plan. A plan we can use any time there's a car outside, with keys in it.'

'Sure you wouldn't rather have it chauffeur-driven?' Gemma said. 'And people with Union Jacks lining the route? Anyhow, you can't drive.'

'I can drive well enough. Anyhow, I know what to do, which pedal to push and all that.'

'So we say "This is a stick-up!" and they all freeze and we belt off into the night in the car you can't drive and Whoopee, we've made it, we're free, just like that?' she said sarcastically.

'No, you're right, Gemma. Right as always. We do it your way. We hand in Little Chum and we don't pull the stick-up or make the break. We just stay here for the rest of our lives—'

'Their faces!' Gemma said. She began to giggle. 'Their faces when you pull out Little Chum! And besides,' she demanded, 'what have we got to lose? Let's give it a try!'

He stared at her. 'Look, which *is* it?' he said. 'Do we or don't we?'

'We do, of course?' Gemma said. 'Yippee!' She danced away. He shook his head wonderingly and followed her.

In a dirty, dusty corner, a breeze blew a piece of paper. It was not the paper with Mo's drawings on it. That had already gone.

That was how Little Chum had been born. An idea, a pile of junk, that became a reality. Now the reality was in his hand, under the bedclothes. Gemma was asleep but Little Chum was wide awake, ready to go.

He pulled the hammer back against its spring. He used an edge of blanket as a muffle, then let the hammer go. It gave a woolly little *clunk*. He smiled, yawned, then fell asleep.

In another bedroom just a few yards along the hall, Kat was not asleep. She sat upright in her bed and frowned at a piece of paper. The paper had drawings on it. They were crude drawings of something long fitted into something wider and shorter. Behind this wider/shorter scribble there was something that could have been a mechanism – or was it just a curved stick ending in a blob? Underneath, there was an outline heavily shaded; a sloping parallelogram.

She had found the drawing in a dirty corner. So if the paper were old, it would have been dirty and dusty too. But it was not. It looked quite new and fresh. That was why she had picked it up.

She turned the paper this way and that. What did the drawing represent? A factory with a chimney? A pop-gun? A microscope? A plan of the garage? The drawing was so crude it could mean almost anything. And yet it suggested *something*. Almost certainly it had been done recently. And done for a purpose. By whom? For what purpose?

She decided to show it to Per in the morning.

In the evening, Michael came back in the car from wherever he had been. Mo raised an eyebrow at Gemma. She nodded grimly and ran to Michael as he climbed from the driving seat.

'Oh, Michael, please!' she cried, hanging on to his arm, 'please, next time you're out, get me a shampoo! I've got to have a shampoo, my hair's disgusting, all claggy and sticky!'

He tried to get rid of her but still she pulled at his arm and thrust her vivid face at him. 'I mean, you've got to go to a town or a village or somewhere with a shop and it wouldn't hurt you to get me a shampoo, just a sachet, any sort!' she clamoured. He mumbled and mouthed, trying to get away.

At last he succeeded and escaped. In his hurry, he left the keys in the car.

'Lovely!' Mo said. 'Well done! What an actress!'

Cautiously, Gemma looked about her to see if they were observed: then ran to the car with Mo. She leaned over the driver's seat and tickled the keys hanging from the dash. 'Jingle bells, jingle bells,' she crooned, jingling them with her fingertip.

'Jingle *all the way*,' Mo said, 'All the way! Tonight! OK?'

'You bet it's OK,' she replied.

CHAPTER TWENTY-TWO

STICK-UP

M o went to the dinner table carrying a folded pile of newspapers and magazines under his arm. They hid Little Chum.

'Get rid of that stuff!' Kat ordered. 'You're here to eat, not to read.' Obediently, Mo tucked the pile between the legs of the chair. Silently he ate the food Kat slapped down before him. Gemma too made herself eat.

The others talked rather bad-temperedly among themselves. 'It's all taking too long!' Macko complained. Mo thought, Oh, I don't know: soon be over, Macko. Just you wait and see! There's a gun under my chair and we've keys for the car waiting outside. Don't be so impatient, Macko!

The meal was over. The men got to their feet, grunted and yawned and made their way to the side table where Gemma had set out the coffee. 'All right,' Kat said. 'Clear away, you two.'

'Clear away?' Mo said. He did not rise from his chair.

'That's what I said,' Kat said, glaring at him.

'Good idea,' Mo said. 'Clear away. Nice thinking.'

Still he did not rise from his chair. Still Kat glared at him. 'Are you trying to be clever, or something?' she said, threateningly.

'Yes!' Mo answered. He reached down under his chair. When he sat up again, the gun was in his hand.

'This is a gun,' he said. 'It's for real. You'd better believe me.' The words sounded good in his ears as he spoke them.

Kat stared at him. The group round the coffee table turned and stared at him. Mo steadied his elbows on the table and pointed the gun at the staring faces.

Gemma was behind Mo now. One of her hands was on his shoulder. 'You told us to clear away,' she said to the kidnappers. Her voice had an edge to it. 'That's just what we're going to do. Try and stop us, and one of you will get hurt. Probably killed.' She looked from face to face expecting to see uncertainty, surprise, even fear. But the faces showed none of these things.

'Real gun, real bullets!' Mo said, trying to make his voice hard and menacing. But there was no response. Everyone just stood there, looking at him expressionlessly.

Macko was the first to crack. Suddenly, amazingly, his legs trembled and gave way under him. He fell to his knees, clasped his hands in front of him and blabbered: 'No! Don't shoot! Not me, don't shoot me!'

Gemma and Mo gaped at him, unable to believe their eyes and ears.

Now Kat fell to pieces. 'You wouldn't shoot me!' she implored. 'Please, let me go!' Her eyes rolled, her face was a piteous mask of terror. I'm a *woman*!' she howled. 'You can't shoot a woman!' She wrung her hands and like Macko, fell to her knees. 'Shoot Michael, shoot Per,' she sobbed, 'but spare my life!'

To Mo and Gemma, it was a fantastic dream. Tough Macko, tough Kat, grovelling, begging . . .

Michael ended the dream. 'That's not fair, Kat,' he said. 'They can't shoot me. I wear spectacles. You're not allowed to hit someone wearing spectacles.' To prove his point, he held out his glasses for Gemma and Mo to inspect – then rapidly replaced them on his nose. 'See!' he said proudly. 'I'm wearing them! Shoot Per!'

'Oh no, not me, I think,' Per said, seriously. 'I have not finished drinking my coffee. Shoot someone else. Macko is good, he is big. A fine target. Shoot Macko.'

Mo said 'Look . . . look, I mean it! This is a real gun loaded with a real bullet!' His voice let him down. It cracked.

Kat, her hard-faced self again, got up from the floor, moved briskly to Mo, stuck out her little finger – and tried to push the tip of it into the barrel of the gun. 'All right then,' she said. 'Fire!'

Whether it was his confusion, or the jerk the gun gave when Kat prodded at it, Mo never knew. All he was certain of was that the spring-loaded hammer slipped from his thumb, which was holding it back; the hammer sprang forward; and the gun fired.

'*Snap*!' it said. A pretty little curl of blue smoke rose above the hammer.

'But . . .' Mo said. 'But – but—'

'But you're not as smart as you think you are,' Kat said. She jerked the gun from Mo's un-resisting fingers and tossed it to Per. He frowned at it, thumbed and snapped the hammer a few times, and handed it to Michael.

Michael examined it at length, pulled a face and said 'This thing's *deadly*. Didn't they teach you kids any physics at school? Here, Macko . . .'

Macko took the gun. He too snapped the hammer. '*Kids*,' he said, shaking his head. 'Just like I told you Michael, it's *dangerous*. All I can say is, good thing Kat found those drawings. Someone could get *hurt* if this went off!'

'Kat found the drawings,' Mo said feebly.

'You left them lying around,' Kat said harshly. '*Stupid*. You made this stupid gun. *Stupid*.'

'It's not stupid,' Mo protested. 'It would work . . .'

'You ought to have your naughty bottoms smacked,' Macko said. He eyed Gemma. She flinched. 'Both of you,' he added, looking hard at Mo. He too flinched.

'I suppose you took the charge out of the bullets,' Mo muttered.

'Too right we did!' Macko said. 'When you were asleep. Kat did it.'

'You and your brilliant secret hiding places!' she said. 'A loose floorboard. Very original, very. And leaving that drawing lying around . . . You really are a pair, you two.' She shook her head wearily.

'What you do, son,' Macko explained to Mo, 'is, just winkle out the bullet from the cartridge – just pull it out – then tap out the propellant, the gunpowder. Then you press the bullet back into the cartridge case. A moron like you wouldn't know the difference.'

'We left the detonator cap alone,' Michael

120

sneered. 'Because it goes off with a nice pop. Like a cap pistol. We thought you'd enjoy hearing your secret weapon go pop!'

'I put everything back in your brilliant secret hiding place,' Kat said, 'and left you to get on with it. Which you did.'

'This is a stick-up!' Macko said, in a TV-cops-and-robber's voice. 'Reach for the ceiling, youse guys! Oh dear. Oh dearie me.'

'The gun would have worked,' Mo said, miserably. 'If you hadn't done things to the bullets—'

'The gun would have blown your stupid head off,' Michael said bleakly.

'But with a proper bullet—'

'Not *bullet*, son, *cartridge*,' Macko said. 'You never learn, do you?'

'Time for beddy-byes,' Kat said. 'Say nighty-night, like good kiddiewinks. And get out.'

Woodenly, Gemma and Mo obeyed. They had to pass the kidnappers to reach the door. As Mo passed Macko, the man grinned and kicked his behind, making him stumble. Gemma too had to pass him. He squeezed her bottom then gave it a loud smack. 'There's my girl!' he said, and winked at her.

In the bedroom, Gemma at once got into bed fully clothed. Mo knew why. She did her best to cry silently, but her bed heaved and creaked for quite a time before she fell asleep.

Mo lay awake, his face burning with shame. Feeling it burn, he cursed himself and told it, 'Go on, then. Burn. You deserved it. You've messed everything up. The gun, the cartridges, the hiding place, leaving the drawing lying around, everything. Burn, face, burn!'

Sleepiness blurred his brain. Ah well, he thought. At least they don't know about the cassette recorder. I've still got that. Maybe, somehow . . .

And the gun. It would have worked, it must have worked, they were wrong about that. It *would* have worked . . .

CHAPTER TWENTY-THREE

RECOIL

'Ah, there you are,' Macko said next morning. Mo tried to get away but the man grabbed his arm and said 'No, this you've got to see. My pleasure, I insist. And where's the Boy Genius's kid sister?'

'Asleep.'

'Well, never mind. Come on, I've got something to show you.'

He had clamped the gun in a bench vice. A long piece of string was tied to the hammer. It led from the gun, round the corner of a wall. 'Your secret weapon,' Macko said, 'we're going to fire it. With a real cartridge up the spout this time. You're going to let it off yourself, you lucky little boy. Come on, cop hold!'

He pushed the free end of the string into Mo's hand. 'Pull it,' he said. 'Pull it nice and slow and gentle, that's the way, till you can feel that the hammer's right back. Hold it steady, don't wobble about.' He clamped his enormous hand over Mo's.

'Now, take this knife,' he ordered. 'It's my knife so you can depend on it to be sharp. I don't mess about like some people. Right, hold steady. When I say "Fire!" you cut the string, right? One quick slice. Got it? OK. Ready . . . steady . . . fire!'

Mo cut the string.

From the unseen place round the corner, there was the sound of a big explosion, immediately followed by a short, whistling scream as some object ricocheted; then tinklings and rattlings as smaller objects fell.

'*Cor!*' Macko said. Then – 'Come on. Let's have a look at your secret weapon.'

They went round the corner and inspected it. Or what was left of it. The breech and the barrel tubes had been forced apart. The chromium-plated barrel, blackened at the firing end, dangled miserably from the bigger tube. There was a lot of smoke. It smelled exciting but Mo felt no excitement.

The hammer and spring had disappeared. 'We've got to find it,' Macko said happily. 'Got to take a good look at it and then have a good think; think what a lucky lad you are, I mean. Come on, don't stand there, help me look.'

Mo unwillingly looked – and happened to find the bit of the gun that had screamed away from the rest. It was the hammer, with a bit of its spring still attached. It was embedded in the wood of some old shelving. Little splinters stuck out like whiskers.

'Ah, so you've found it!' Macko said. 'Looks nice doesn't it, stuck in that wood? Very nice effect. Sort of modern sculpture, like. Do you know how it got there? Well, do you?'

Mo muttered 'Yes', and wished himself dead.

'Right, then,' Macko said. 'Explain it to me. Tell me all about it. Go on.'

'The cartridge was fired,' Mo said, 'and the force of the explosion drove the bullet through the barrel—'

'Knocking the barrel and breech apart as it went on its merry way,' Macko said. 'But we mustn't let little things like that worry us, must we?' The other kidnappers entered. They stood watching and listening. Macko welcomed this audience. Mo did not.

'I'm taking lessons in engineering from the boy genius,' Macko said. 'Right, the front end of your secret weapon blew apart. What happened at the other end? Go on, tell us.'

'There was a recoil,' Mo muttered.

'Ah, a recoil!' Macko said. 'Ten out of ten for that! A recoil, yes definitely! The cartridge case shot backwards, didn't it, you silly boy? It went backwards, oh yes it did, very fast indeed! And what would have happened, you backward boy, if you had been holding that secret weapon of yours in your hand when the naughty cartridge exploded?'

'Got injured,' Mo said.

'Injured,' Macko said. 'Well, I suppose you could put it that way. You'd have got injured. Perhaps your thumb would have been torn off. And your upper arm smashed. Or perhaps your eye would have been whipped out if you'd been fool enough to have sighted the gun. Well?'

Mo said nothing.

'Well, say something!' Macko shouted. He seized Mo's hair and jerked his head back so that Mo had to look into his face; a face filled with clumsy triumph, the face of a playground bully with a small boy at his mercy. Mo despised the face. But he despised himself still more.

'Say "I'm a silly boy"!' Macko shouted. Now Mo's eyes were beginning to water. He was not crying. It was the hair-pulling. But they'd think it was tears, they'd think he was crying. . .

'Say it!' Macko shouted.

'Silly boy . . .' Mo whispered, thinking, Tears, they'll all think it's tears.

Per saved him. 'That is enough, I think,' he told Macko. 'Let him go. Now I am speaking to him. Listen, Mo, listen very carefully while I am

126

talking to you. There are things you do not understand. You do not think we are serious. But we are serious. You are not to be let to escape, do you understand that?

'And guns, and being clever. You do not understand about guns, but Macko does. We all do. You do not understand that you are only a boy, not so clever. But that is the truth. You and your sister, you are children. You are to do what you are told and be good children. That is all you are to do. No escapings and silly tricks. You understand?'

Mo said 'Yes' and worried about his eyes. If he wiped them, everyone would think he was wiping away tears. If he did not wipe them, everyone would see the water that looked like tears. This seemed to him far more important than anything Per had said.

Kat said, 'Where is she, that sister of yours? Upstairs and still in bed? Well, turf her out. Get her down here, she's got to attend to our other gormless captive. Shave his woolly whiskers and that. Go on, now. And behave yourself.'

Mo moved to the staircase. His hands felt huge and his head seemed inflated. Nothing of him seemed to fit, he did not know how to carry himself. Their eyes seemed to project rods that stiffened his joints.

He tripped on a stair. 'Mind your step!' Macko called after him and guffawed. Oh, ha-ha, Mo thought, funny joke, just about your level, you great ape. But the joke's on me, the joke's on me . . .

At last he reached the bedroom. He closed the door behind him and leaned against it. Now he was alone, except for Gemma. She lay sleeping. He had to face her, talk to her, hide his feelings from her. What he wanted was to throw himself on his bed and yell into his pillow.

She woke, glanced at his face and saw everything. She was careful to look away when she spoke to him. 'They've been having fun?' she asked in a low voice. 'I heard a bang. The gun, I suppose. I suppose they've been—'

'They've been sending me up,' he said. 'And you've been awake all the time. You weren't asleep.'

She did not answer. Mo tried to say something but could only make a choking noise.

'It's all right, Mo,' Gemma said. 'Honest it is! We'll show them! We'll still show them!'

Mo got hold of himself. 'There's one thing we *won't* show them, Gem,' he said. He felt better. Now he could bear Gemma looking at him. 'It's something special. They don't know about it. Listen, Gem . . .'

He told her about the hidden cassette recorder. She listened, with big dark eyes staring, admiring eyes. Of course they were admiring. He spoke faster and faster, feeling better every moment.

When he had finished, Gemma spoke.

'You've got to be mad!' she said. 'Stupid, crazy, mad!'

He gaped at her, amazed. But then Kat yelled at them and he had no time to reply or understand.

CHAPTER TWENTY-FOUR

THE TELEPHONE CALL

'But why?' Gemma said when they were locked in their bedroom for the night. 'How stupid can you get! Why steal it? You'll get your head knocked off your shoulders by Kat, just you wait and see.'

Mo looked miserably at the tape recorder. Why *had* he taken it? Because it was a nice old thing, really vintage, lots of knobs and buttons and digital read-outs . . . was that why? There ought to be a better reason.

'You and your gadgets!' Gemma said, disgustedly. 'You're like a baby reaching out for a coloured rattle! Oo, oo, gug, gug, I *want* it, I *want* it!'

'I'll give it back,' Mo said. He felt defeated.

'You can't, you moron. We're locked in till morning. Honestly!'

She got into bed and went to sleep. Mo stared dully at the tape recorder for a long time; so long that he heard Michael leave in the car, and Macko get into his bed, and Kat thumping about putting things away. Tomorrow she would be thumping him.

If only the door were unlocked! But it never was. Kat never forgot. He made his way silently to the door, gently turned the handle and pulled, very cautiously.

Kat, who never forgot, had forgotten. The door opened. He tiptoed into the dark, unable to believe his luck. He could put the tape recorder back!

There was a corner of the long deserted garage that still bore the sign OFFICE. As Mo crept down the stairs, keeping to the edge of the treads to avoid making them creak, this sign showed palely in the darkness. It was Mo's beacon, the only pointer to where he was heading. He kept his eye on it—

And suddenly the grey glow went out, extinguished like a light: then glowed again.

Someone was down there. Someone's body had passed between him and the sign. Mo's heart stopped – jumped to life again – then thumped inside him. He froze.

Now there were sounds, so faint that he could not make them out. Gentle sounds, *'gurr . . . gurr . . . gurr'*. And lights or rather, a light. The light glimmered for a second and went out. Glimmered again and went out.

Then, very quietly, almost in a whisper, seeming right beside him, a voice spoke. 'Hello,' it said, hollowly. 'Hello, hello.'

The voice seemed to be speaking to him! Mo put his hand over his mouth to stop himself answering. The voice could not be for him, it was impossible . . .

And so it proved. For now the voice was speaking again and Mo recognized it. Per. It was Per, speaking on the telephone. The strange sounds had been Per dialling. He must have had a cushion over the handset to dull the noise. And the light must have been a little torch flashed on so that Per could see the numbers.

'Yes,' said Per's voice. 'Yes, that is right . . . Yes, you are dealing only with me. Only with me, you understand? It does not concern the others. This is private, between us, you understand? . . . So. Good, yes, a gentleman's agreement, as you say. Yes, two hundred thousand pounds. That is the agreed ransom for your PC Blowers. Yes, he is in excellent health and will remain so providing that – yes, providing you pay the money. Two hundred thousand . . . To my bank account in Switzerland, you understand. I give you the bank account numbers now, yes? You take them down. 1437, you have that? Good. Next—'

Mo had been leaning forward to overhear. All

his weight was on one foot. Beneath his foot, a rotting board shifted perhaps a millimetre, yet the noise – *'Gack!'* – was frightful.

Mo heard Per gasp and say, 'Wait!' into the telephone. There was a long and awful silence. Mo could feel Per's eyes, like black searchlight beams, raking the darkness, looking for him. His heart thudded so loudly that Per must hear . . .

Per did not. 'Hello . . . hello . . .' he said and continued his conversation.

Mo crept upstairs, an inch at a time, to his bed. He had forgotten about returning the stolen tape recorder. Safe in bed, he found that he was still clutching it. He cursed himself, then lay rigid and wide awake, trying to work out what he had heard and what to do about it.

Soon it was all clear to him. He slept, smiling in his sleep. In the morning he talked with Gemma about Per's double-dealing. She took it well.

At breakfast, there was the expected fuss about the tape recorder. Where had it gone? Someone had taken it. Who?

'Me,' Mo admitted. Kat snatched the machine from him and gave one of her best slaps across the face.

'Why did you take it?'

'Just to look at. Just to play with. It's a nice old one—'

Another slap. Per said, 'Do not do that.' Kat snorted and left them. Now Mo and Gemma were alone with Per. He said, 'It is very wicked to steal.' He prodded the recorder's control tabs. 'At least you have done no damage, I think. No, wait! Where is the cassette? The tape?'

'Ah, the tape,' Mo said. 'Well, you see, I heard something in the night; and I had the tape recorder—'

'So he used it,' Gemma said.

Per's face seemed to change. It aged and glazed as they watched it. His voice sounded choked. 'You must tell me—'

'About last night?' Mo said.

'Funny things happened last night,' Gemma said. 'Such a coincidence! I mean, someone making a telephone call in the middle of the night—'

'A secret call,' Mo said. 'And there I was with the tape recorder. Terrific coincidence. Very sensitive microphone, that tape recorder has.'

Per's face was very white and shining with the film of sweat. 'Give me that tape,' he said.

'Lost it,' Mo said, innocently.

Per gripped Mo's wrist so hard that bones creaked. 'Give it to me!' he said, almost in a gasp.

'Wasting your time, Per,' Gemma said. She stared at Per in a new, cold way. The old, doting look was completely gone.

'But you don't understand . . .' Per began, letting go Mo's wrist.

'Oh yes we do,' Mo said. 'Two hundred thousand pounds. All for you.'

'No one but you,' Gemma said. 'All for yourself. No sharing. In a Swiss bank account. It's all on the tape.'

'Give me the tape!' Per said. 'If you don't—'

'If we don't?' Gemma said, acidly sweet. 'What will you do if we don't?'

'Tell the others?' Mo suggested. 'Tell them, "There's a tape missing. Please all join in and help me find it!" '

'But then you'd have to tell them what you're searching for,' Gemma said. 'And if you didn't tell them, we would. We'd tell Macko first. Macko with the big muscles. Wonder what he'd think? Wonder what he'd do?'

'He might ask for his share of the two hundred thousand pounds,' Gemma suggested in a sweet voice.

Per choked out something and almost ran up the stairs. 'He's going to search our bedroom,' Mo grinned. 'He won't find anything. Poor old Per.'

135

'Poor people, suffering people, oppressed people,' Gemma said, rolling her eyes. 'We fight for them.' She had suddenly remembered Per's words when they were first kidnapped. Then, his words had stirred her. Now they were a sick joke.

Above them, there were frantic yet carefully subdued noises as Per searched for the tape that could reveal his treachery to the rest of the gang. Gemma began to giggle. Mo tried to shush her, but caught the giggles too. Kat heard and came in. 'What's the big joke?' she demanded.

'Nothing!' Gemma said.

'Nothing!' said Mo.

They spoke the truth. The big joke was – nothing. There was nothing on the tape. Mo had never used the machine to record. Had Per found the cassette – but that was impossible, Mo had thrown it into the depths of a tub filled with ancient sump oil – there would have been nothing for him to hear except a long, blank hiss filled with his own fear and guilt.

CHAPTER TWENTY-FIVE

THE DEMOLITION JOB

N ow the gang had completely lost direction. D & C, Divide and Conquer, had done its work.

Per the leader was no longer capable of leading. His mind was chained to the single, hopeless mystery of the missing tape. Macko, knowing that something had gone wrong and nothing was going right, swore and blustered. 'Where's Michael?' he complained. 'When are we getting some *action*?' Kat glowered and banged things about, scorning Macko and hating Per. Gemma and Mo, sweet and sour by turns, kept everyone at everyone else's throats.

PC Blowers remained an island of quiet. He was like a sheep waiting to be sold at market, unambitious, uncomplaining, uninterested.

But then there was a car outside: and footsteps; and Michael hurried in. 'It's on!' he said. 'It's all fixed! Get those kids out and I'll tell you!'

Mo and Gemma listened through the floor-boards. It was a complicated plan – hired cars, meeting points, safe conduct, a waiting aeroplane with Per at the controls – and they could not hear much of it. But, 'Tomorrow it will all be over!' Gemma whispered, hugging herself.

'And they'll get everything they wanted,' Mo said bitterly. 'The money, everything. They'll have won.'

The day of liberation began in the middle of the night. Their bedroom door was flung open, the light glared rawly as Kat switched it on and – 'Downstairs, you brats!' she said. Mo and Gemma rubbed their eyes and obeyed.

Everyone was there, Michael, Per, Kat, Macko. Only Macko seemed at ease. The rest muttered to each other, checked the contents of briefcases and did the same things twice. Kat slopped mugs of coffee at Mo and Gemma and said, 'Drink up. Then you can kiss me farewell. Partings are such sweet sorrow, I don't think.'

'Aren't you going to give me a final slap?' Gemma said, viciously. 'Just one more for the road?' Kat raised her hand. Macko held it. 'Don't mark them,' he said. 'What's the point? Got to deliver them all nice and shiny. Like new. Same for our boy in blue, Puffer Blowers. Give him his shave, Gemma. Make him look lovely, the stupid great oik.'

Gemma went to shave Puffer. While she rubbed shaving cream into his whiskers she heard an unfamiliar car engine outside. She supposed it to be one of the hire cars the gang talked of. There were last-minute shouts and reminders and the car's doors slammed. 'That's Kat and Per gone,' she said, half to herself and half to Puffer. Puffer nodded his big, mild head and drank the half-cup of coffee she had saved for him. She had to hold it for him, of course; his hands were, as always, bound behind his back—

But they weren't!

As she touched the razor to his face, the blade nicked him. He started and automatically raised one hand in front of him. Amazed, she looked behind his back. Only his hands kept the cable taut. He held one end of it and had dropped the other. He muttered, 'Quick! In my hand!'

Michael and Macko stood only a few yards away. She did not dare speak out loud. She put the loose end in his hand and whispered, 'What's happening, what are you up to?' He replied, 'That coffee's *hot*. Could be useful.' She looked into his eyes, trying to understand what he could mean. His eyes had changed. There was something hard and urgent in them. 'Hot coffee,' he said. 'Wait till I tell you, then . . .' He made a sort of sideways swipe with his head. She finished shaving him, still not understanding him.

Now Michael started his car, she could hear it outside. Macko shouted, 'Off, then? Take it easy, mind!' The engine revved and Michael said something. Macko replied, 'Yeah, see you there, where the palm trees wave! Can't wait! Take it easy, now!' The car went away.

They were alone with Macko.

Macko enjoyed the situation. He paraded himself and his sawn-off shotgun, walking back and forth, flexing his muscles, talking louder and faster. 'Crime doesn't pay, that's what they tell you,' he said, grinning. 'Well, let *me* tell *you*, you kids – and *you*, flatfoot – that they've got it all wrong. One hundred per cent wrong. You know your arithmetic, sonny?' he asked Mo. 'Well, you work this little sum out. A million pounds divided by four. Go on, work it out! See what you get! 'Cause that's what I'm getting! And I know how to spend it! And where!'

'Can I have my exercise?' Puffer asked mildly. 'I've got cramp.'

'Right, get him up on his feet,' Macko told Gemma. 'Walk him about a bit. Get your muscles working, copper. You never know, one day you might get the chance for another ding-dong with old Macko! Would you like that? I would! Be lovely, it would!'

Puffer meekly walked back and forth, hands behind his back. Then – 'Car!' he said, stopping in mid-stride and staring at Gemma. His eyes! Again, they seemed to her to have a new look in them, a hardness. 'Car, what car?' she said. 'Thought I heard a car coming,' Puffer replied, vaguely. 'I'll look,' Mo said.

Macko beat him to the window – thrust him aside. Now Gemma understood. Talk of a car had excited Macko. He peered out of the window, forgetting Gemma, forgetting Puffer, forgetting everything but the mysterious car. 'Drink coffee!' Puffer muttered to Gemma. Baffled, she filled her cup from the pot on the stove.

Mo and Macko were looking out of the window; so only Gemma saw what happened in the next few seconds. Puffer standing bound, wrists behind his back: Puffer suddenly unbound, arms free! Then impossibly, Puffer in mid air, a sort of human jet plane!

The crown of his head slammed into Macko's back. Macko's head went through the window. He gave a great shout and staggered back and away, blood pouring from cuts on his scalp. He was appalled by the blood – his own precious blood! – and dazed. But he still gripped the gun.

'Coffee!' yelled Puffer as he launched himself once again. Now Gemma knew what to do. She flung her mug of hot coffee at Macko's head. It hit Macko at the same instant that Puffer's head hit him, this time in the midriff. Macko staggered back, pawing at the blood and coffee covering his face. He tripped and sat down heavily, gun in hand.

Mo took his chance: he jumped on the gun and stood on it, trusting to his weight to pin it and Macko's hand to the floor.

Macko grunted and effortlessly lifted the hand that held the gun. Mo went flying, his mouth an O.

To Gemma's horror, Puffer let Macko get up. Macko stood legs spread, holding the gun like a club. His eyes were confident and wicked. 'Right, then!' he grated, swinging the gun by its barrel, swinging it slowly like the head of a snake about to strike. 'All right, copper! Come on!'

Puffer came on, moving as slowly and deliberately as the swinging gun. As he advanced, he said over his shoulder, 'You two kids – *out*!' There was a whiplash edge to his voice that made them obey. They backed to the door and stood there, hypnotized. '*Out*!' Puffer repeated. They left the garage and went to the broken window.

Staring through it, they witnessed a demolition job.

They saw the gun swing and Puffer catch the hands that swung it. Then Puffer seemed to fall sideways, easily and deliberately, and Macko's great body was suddenly hurtling above the floor to land thunderously on a wooden table. The table crashed into splinters. Now Puffer had the gun.

He had the gun but did not want it. He threw it away from him as if it were something that got in his way, a toy, an inconvenience. 'He's mad!' Mo gasped. Without the gun, the two men were on equal terms.

Macko glared, grunted – and flung himself at Puffer, hands spread to grasp his throat. Puffer made a gentle wiping motion with his left arm, sweeping the grasping hands aside. His right hand chopped down and his right knee came up in Macko's throat. Macko screamed hoarsely and sprawled on hands and knees, mouth gaping.

'Well, come on, then,' Puffer said, mildly. Quietly, he watched Macko, his eyes still murderous, reassemble himself. 'When you're ready,' Puffer said, conversationally.

Macko came in punching. The great arms swung, the hammer fists battered. Puffer let himself be hit, once, twice; then walked into the blows – walked inside them, so that the two men were body to body, face against face. Puffer did something so quick that neither Mo nor Gemma saw what it was; something to Macko's back; something that left him on the floor arching and writhing, face twisted, legs thrashing.

Gemma hid her face in her hands and gave a muffled scream. Puffer heard. He glanced at her, looked down at the sobbing Macko and said, 'Well, enough's enough, I suppose.' He sounded reluctant.

Then he sat down on a wooden chair, took off a shoe and began talking to it.

CHAPTER TWENTY-SIX

FREEDOM

So many things happened so fast that Gemma and Mo could not keep up. Police cars. Policemen asking questions. Police photographers.

Glimpses of a police van with, so they were told, Per, Kat and Michael inside.

Am ambulance for Macko – 'My back, my back . . .'

The screech of tyres as the Embassy Rolls, recklessly driven by their father, lurched to a halt outside and their parents ran in, hugging and kissing and questioning them.

The questions were easy enough to answer when they were about plain facts. But some of the questions puzzled Gemma and Mo at the time; and for a long time after.

For example: their mother said 'Do you hate them very much? Because you must try not to, hate is such a waste. Try not to, won't you?'

'But . . .' Mo began, and did not know how to go on. The gang had been the enemy. What they had done was wicked and often brutal. Did he hate them? He had never thought about it before. He tried to switch the conversation to another track with a joke. 'Old Gemma certainly didn't hate Per!' he said. 'Far from it! All starry-eyed!' As he spoke the words, he felt them fall dead and flat. Gemma slammed them into the ground.

'Per!' she said, viciously. 'That's the only one I do hate! Lying, rotten, phoney—'

'Gemma!' her mother said, shocked by her daughter's venom. She recovered herself and said 'That's just what I mean. Hate is so—'

'But Gemma's right, I know just what she means,' Mo said. 'He was the worst because he was rotten. Rotten at the centre like – you know, an apple with bugs in it, all shiny outside and rotten inside.'

'But Per wasn't the one that *hit* you, *ill-treated* you,' his mother said.

'No, not us, he didn't hurt us,' Mo agreed, unwillingly.

'He's the sort of person who hurts the *world*,' Gemma said, violently yet feebly. The words were wrong, she knew. Yet she also knew that the thought was right.

'But Kat and that big man, Macko,' their father said. 'Vicious! Cruel! A violent great brute!

'Old Kat was all right really,' Gemma said.

Unconsciously, she stroked the cheek that Kat had so often slapped.

'But she hit you! She constantly hit you, slapped you!'

'Thought you didn't want us to hate anyone,' Mo muttered, feeling more confused than ever.

Gemma said 'Don't you see, she couldn't really *help* it, she was *angry* inside, because she'd *tried*, she'd *been* there! . . .' However much pressure she pumped into her words, they had no effect. Her parent's handsome, sympathetic, uncomprehending faces told her that.

Mo and Gemma couldn't explain about Macko, either. 'If he'd been a farmhand, or something, instead of a kidnapper,' Gemma began.

'He was just a sort of a *kid*,' Mo continued. 'School-bully sort of person. Showing off to himself and anyone who'd take any notice. I wouldn't say he was really bad, he just did bad things.'

He saw his father's eyebrows go up and his mouth purse. Mo wasn't surprised. Obviously his own words sounded like nonsense. But were they nonsense? Mo thought, I don't know.

Now Gemma tried to bring in a lighter touch. 'None of us is perfect,' she said, brightly and primly. Her attempt, like Mo's, failed. She hurried on to say 'Michael was sort of a kid too,

I suppose. He'd got this great idea, this theory about things, but he hadn't worked it all out, he didn't know what he was organizing *for . . .*'

Mo thought, They weren't there, my father and mother, that's the trouble. So how can they understand? They want me and Gemma to be perfect – we're the goodies, the gang are the baddies. But it wasn't like that.

Aloud, he said 'Can I have just one more Coke?' His father said 'Sure.' Mo drank some of it. He said 'Gemma was all right, she really was! Real old tiger, you should have seen her!'

Gemma, not hearing Mo and still trying to sort out her thoughts, said 'They were all vain, that's it, vain. Vain about different things. Vain, or jealous, or wanting something they could never have. Lots of people are like that. But not me, of course,' she added, putting on an act. 'I'm *perfect*.' She did clownish things with her head.

'You and your pashes!' Mo said, grinning.

'You and your gadgets!' she replied.

She became serious again. 'They were each in a dream,' she said, 'and all the dreams were different. And a bit stupid.' She shrugged and said 'I used to hang on to Mo. He was real.' She leaned over and patted him on the head. '*Good* boy,' she said, in her nursery voice of years ago. '*Good* big brudderkins!'

'Rotten gunmaker,' he said ruefully. He still brooded over Little Chum.

But then he discovered that she had taken his Coke and briefly they were truly back in the old days, the days before the snatch, the days when they were young.

It was not until two days later that they had the chance to talk, more or less alone, with Puffer. It was an Official Occasion. Puffer was a strange sight in his dark blue, awkward-looking suit; out of place among all the sleek officials and handsomely uniformed senior Police Officers; gloomy.

'Go on, cheer up!' Gemma told him. 'After all, you're the big hero!'

'*They* don't think so,' Puffer said. 'Seems I'm up for a telling-off. Official reprimand, you know the sort of thing.'

'What do you mean, telling-off? Whatever for?'

'Duffing up that Macko. They say I used "unnecessary force". *I* don't know . . .'

'But he'd have *shot* you, *killed* you!—'

'Well, there you are. Try telling *them* that!'

'I will,' Gemma said – and flounced away, nose high. She buttonholed the most important-looking person present and lectured him at the top of her voice. The important person backed away, nervously nodding agreement and spilling his sherry.

Mo watched, smiling. 'She'll fix it,' he said. Puffer nodded and grinned. 'Fix anything between the two of you,' he said. 'You acted smart all through. Very smart. Did just the right things. Got them so they didn't know if they were coming or going. A treat to watch.' He stroked his large, bruised chin. 'Mind you, I didn't exactly enjoy just sitting there, watching, all that time . . .'

'We were wondering about that, Gemma and I,' Mo said. 'Why did you leave it to the very end? I mean, you must have known all along that you could take any of them, all of them.'

'Not safe,' Puffer replied. 'They'd got guns and that. Guns go off, people get hurt. My instructions were, Safety of the Children First. Couldn't take any risks. And besides—'

'Besides, you'd taken a sort of dislike to Macko?' Gemma said. She had finished off the important person.

'Well, there was that,' Puffer said. 'Mind you, the big ones aren't much trouble usually. It's the little scrawny ones you have to watch out for. In pubs. They can turn out terrors. And *women*. Oh dear, oh dear, the women! When I was in the Force—'

'Ah!' Gemma pounced. 'So you're not in the

Force! Not a policeman at all! I thought so! You're—'

'That Macko, you see, he wasn't *trained*,' Puffer said, earnestly. 'He's a big lad, I grant you that, but muscles aren't enough. You've got to be *trained*.'

'You're not a policeman at all,' Gemma insisted. 'I know what you are! You're SAS! Aren't you?'

'SAS?' Puffer said. 'Ah, I've heard of them. Sort of Specials.' He gave her a deliberately blank and sheep-like stare.

Gemma puffed out her breath despairingly and gave up. 'Well, at least tell about your children,' she said. 'When you crashed in that night and let them capture you, you said, "I've got kids of my own"—'

Puffer smiled. 'Right bit of play-acting that was,' he said. 'Blundering about, doing everything all wrong. Went against the grain. Still, it had to be done that way. Had to get in somehow, to keep an eye on you two. But I felt a proper clown.'

'About your children,' Gemma reminded him. 'How many? How old?'

'That was a bit more play-acting,' Puffer said. 'I haven't got any kids. Not married or anything. Don't go much for kids, as a matter of fact. Present company excepted, of course,' he added, gallantly.

'Never mind that, what about the shoe?' Mo said impatiently.

'What shoe?'

'You kept talking to your *shoe*. I thought you were mad, we both did.'

'Oh, my *shoe*,' Puffer said. 'Ah, that's clever, that shoe. Is anyone looking at us? No? . . .' He took off his shoe. 'You like gadgets,' he told Mo. 'You'll like this!'

He swung the rubber of the heel aside. In the hollow of the heel there nestled tiny metal boxes, ceramic pimples, glittering drums.

'Radio transmitter!' Mo said.

'And receiver. Two-way. Very handy,' Puffer said. 'And there's a sort of bug too. So I was able to keep the authorities informed all along, you see. Tell them what the plans were, when things would happen, everything. Very clever piece of apparatus. Miniaturized.'

'How did you plant the bug?' Mo said.

'Oh, the night I arrived. When that Macko fellow worked me over. I planted it under the big table during the schemozzle.'

'But how *could* you have done! How did you find *time*?' Gemma said. 'He was knocking you about all over the place! Your poor face—'

'Ah, well,' Puffer said. 'You don't take much notice of amateurs trying to mess you about. They're not *trained*.'

His face was mild and earnest. Gemma kissed it.

'And you haven't got any children and you're not married,' she said, musingly.

Oh Lord, Mo thought. She's Off Again.

Gary Paulsen
Hatchet

*There was almost no light when he opened his eyes again.
The darkness of night was thick and for a moment he began
to panic . . . The world came back. He was still in pain, all-
over pain . . .*

When a thirteen-year-old city boy crash lands into the
Canadian wilderness, all he is left with is a hatchet – and the
need to survive. From now on he learns everything the hard
way . . .

'A heart-stopping story . . . something beyond adventure.'
Publishers Weekly

'A spellbinding winner.'
Kirkus Reviews

A 1988 NEWBERY HONOR BOOK